HOME & HEARTH

Southern Stories/Family Recipes by
MABLE ELIZABETH GATES

INTRODUCTION+DESIGN BY LELA RAST HARTSAW

Featuring her 1994 prize-winning
Memories of Mississippi essay, The Country Doctor, reprinted
here with permission of the copyright holder.

Copyright by
Lela Rast Hartsaw

WHAT'S MAMA WRITING PRESS
whatsmamawriting@gmail.com

Copyright © 2021 WMW PRESS
All rights reserved.
ISBN: 978-1-7369652-0-7

DEDICATION

This volume of original stories and family recipes is dedicated to those who have gone before us, those we love today, and those who will follow us in the years to come.

Introduction

It is an honor and a joy to have been allowed to gather into one book, the writings by my maternal grandmother's sister even if I am left to ponder what to call her—is she my *great* aunt or my *grand* aunt? Both monikers seem awkward. Mable Elizabeth Gates has always simply been 'Aunt Mable' to me and when I read her stories, I am lucky to hear them in her distinct, sweet southern voice. But one doesn't need to hear Mable's voice in their head to enjoy her storytelling. Her talent lies in her ability to share her evocative imagination and keen memory through faithful descriptions and details.

These original stories capture the spirit of life in the 20th century American South. It was a time when folks relied on one another and tight-knit circles were strong because of this unity. In these rural communities, a person or family in need was cared for without hesitation, like in *Son of the Heart* and there was powerful peace in the presence of neighbors stepping in after a tragedy like in *Night of Terror*. Mable's tale of generational love between a grandfather and his granddaughter in *Harvest of Love* is a tender homage to this familial bond and simpler times.

Some of Mable's stories, like *Shady Grove Civil War Nurse,* were once published in the local newspaper. Her tale of the beloved house calls made by Dr. Windham in *The Country Doctor*, won a special place in the archives at the University of Mississippi which held a writing contest in 1994 asking for stories written about the Great Depression in Mississippi by those who had experienced it. My Aunt Mable's heartwarming account of the remarkable dedication to his community by Dr. Windham is part of the University Museums collection *Memories of Mississippi,* and is reprinted here with permission.

Included in this book is a collection of lost family recipes. Some are savory, but apparently, we liked sweets because somehow there are twice as many recipes for the dessert section. I hope you'll try a few. Lela's Chicken + Dumplings are divine and the Chocolate Cobbler from Aunt Linda is a crowd-pleaser.

Lela's biscuits, her from-scratch version of a Southern kitchen staple, were regarded as some of the best around. For fun, I did a little biscuit math and determined that since she married at the age of 13 (in 1919) and passed away at the age of 74 (in 1980), even with subtracting ten years to account for the days when one of her girls made the biscuits for the day and the years late in life when she most likely didn't make them, Lela Cooper Myrick still baked approximately 200,000 biscuits in her lifetime.

My hope is that by collecting, preserving, and publishing these stories and recipes, many more people will have the opportunity to enjoy Mable's ability to transport her readers to another place and time. This collection will allow others to enjoy the food that was lovingly prepared and shared by women in the family as well as meet the people that live on in Mable's vivid memories, now captured in print for generations to come.

Lela Hartsaw

Lela Rast Hartsaw
Author of *The Adventure of Abigail Rose—Ida Patten's Antebellum Doll* and *Abigail Rose Visits Gamble Plantation*

PS. Special thanks to my husband, Mike Hartsaw, for understanding the need for "Chair Time" to get this project complete. And extra special thanks to my mother, Brenda Dowdy Bell, for gently nudging me through a pandemic, surgery, illness, and all the other potholes & hurdles. xoxo

CONTENTS

NIGHT OF TERROR..11

CHARLIE MYRICK ENTERS THE SERVICE................................29

THE COUNTRY DOCTOR..33

HARVEST OF LOVE..39

DADDY'S LOVE GAVE ME STRENGTH......................................55

SON OF THE HEART..59

SHADY GROVE CIVIL WAR NURSE..79

COOPER FAMILY HISTORY..83

LOST FAMILY RECIPES..99
RECIPE INDEX..123

Southern Stories/Family Recipes by
MABLE ELIZABETH GATES

and asked, "Catching anything, boys?"

When Charlie turned to answer him, his line was jerked so hard he almost fell into the river. "Help, Joe," he hollered. Both boys pulled on the cane pole as hard as they could.

The lawman dismounted to see if he could help. Just as he got to the edge of the water, both boys fell backward. A large catfish flew through the air and landed in the grass near them.

The deputy laughed and said, "I don't think you boys need my help, so I'll be going." He mounted his horse and rode away as the boys took the big catfish off Charlie's hook and ran a string through its gills. They tied the string to a nearby tree keeping the catfish in the shallow water so it would not die.

They sat, talking as they fished. Joe asked Charlie if he liked the lawman. "I guess so," he answered. "Do you?" Joe turned a troubled face to Charlie and said, "I don't like him much. He hangs around our house too much, and he is always trying to put his hands on Mary—him with a wife and a little girl."

When the time came to go home, they had caught a nice string full of catfish. They divided them so each family would have a mess. They parted company at the fork in the road, and each one went toward his house. Charlie called his brother Jim to come help him scale the big fish. Jim said, "Dang, Charlie, this thing weighs ten pounds." "I know," Charlie replied. "Now you can have all you want to eat."

Joe trudged slowly home with his catch. As he got near the back door, his brother John came out with the milk buckets. When

Night of Terror

The two ragged urchins sat on the bank of the river, their cane poles dangling in the water below. The warm March sun danced off the swift running waves. It was the hour past noon, and a good time to bring the big cats up to catch the insects that hovered near the surface of the water.

As they sat enjoying the warm day and the companionship of being together, they heard the drawing of a horse's hooves on the hard dirt road.

Joe sat with his back to a big beach tree and shielded his eyes from the strong sunlight. He said, "Hey, Charlie, ain't that Deputy Dellinger?"

Charlie squinted toward the sound of the running horse. "Yeah, I think it is. It looks like his roan."

As the lawman came abreast of them, he reined in his horse

he saw Joe's catch he said, "Oh, boy, fish for supper." He called for their mother to bring some pliers and knives and a pan of water.

They took the fish to the wash bench under the trees and started to skin them. Mattie Brawner stood watching her sons as they cleaned the fish. She was a tall, thin woman with graying hair that she wore in a neat bun low on her neck. At one time she might have been considered pretty, but time and hard work and too much sun from working long hours in the fields turned her old before her time.

She smiled as she patted Joe on the head. "We knew you and Charlie was having good luck. Deputy Dellinger told us you were fishing the Obine River run."

Joe looked at the tired, careworn face of his mother and asked, "What did he want?"

"He said he just stopped by to see how we were to ask if we had seen any strangers around. Seems there have been some things stolen on the Essary farm, down the road."

Joe and John finished cleaning the fish, and Mattie took them toward the kitchen door. She turned and said, "You boys hurry with the feeding and milking, I'll have these catfish fried when you get back, with lots of biscuits and gravy."

The Brawner farm was one of the best kept in the area. Will Brawner took pride in keeping everything neat and in good repair.

That winter he had built a new tobacco barn. The old one had been torn down and some of the wood used to repair the other buildings around the farm. On Saturdays Joe and John had white washed all the buildings and repaired all the fences. On that Saturday Will and John had burned a place and prepared a box to sow the tobacco seeds.

The tired, hungry family gathered around the table for supper. Mattie, Mary, and Sarah placed plates of fried catfish, biscuits and gravy in the center of the table. After eating, Will rose and went into the back room where Mattie had placed the wash tub for his bath. One after the other, they each took a bath and went to bed. Church services were at 9 o'clock, and will Brawner was not one to be late.

In the next few weeks the ground was ready for planting an early corn and gardens.

On April 18, the worst earthquake to hit the United States since 1811 almost destroyed San Francisco. It happened at 5:15 in the morning, just as the city was waking for the day.

All the newspapers carried stories and pictures of the death and destruction. Deputy Dellinger used this excuse to come to the Brawner farm to show them the newspapers. He would ride out almost every day with a new story.

Joe and Charlie had constructed a boat out of some old wood and used tar and pitch to caulk the seams. When they decided it was safe to put it into the river, they drifted to a place no one ever went. There were no roads or paths. The only way was by water, and they went there to hunt. When they were smaller, they had made friends with an old Indian who lived deep in the woods. They had met Lone Eagle one winter day while they were hunting.

He had a brace of quail, two wild turkeys, and some rabbits he had killed.

At first, they were so frightened, they could not run. Lone Eagle stood staring at the two boys. He reached toward them and said, "I your friend."

Charlie finally swallowed his fear enough to say, "We your friends."

The Indian could see the boys had not had any luck that day. He took two rabbits, some quail, and one of the wild turkeys and gave them to the boys. As he picked up the other game and turned to leave, he said "You know tell you see me. You come here again, I help you hunt."

All that winter Charlie and Joe had returned to the same place, and Lone Eagle always came and showed them where to hunt. He showed them how to make snares to catch birds and the big swamp rabbits that were so plentiful in the river bottom.

One winter day they paddled their boat to the same place. They tied it to a tree and walked into the woods. They had not gone far when it began to snow big wet flakes. Soon their clothes were soaked and they were shivering from the cold. It was snowing so hard they could not see their way back to the boat. Just as they begin to be scared that they were lost, Lone Eagle appeared out of the swirling blanket of white.

"Foolish boys, you come with me," he said. So they came to a small shack. The Indian opened the door and nudged them inside.

A roaring fire was burning in the fireplace. They ran toward it and stuck their hands out to its warmth. Lone Eagle went to the bunk fastened to one wall and came back with two blankets. "You take clothing off to dry, wrap in this."

When their clothing had been hung to dry by the fire, Lone Eagle brought two bowls and dipped in the pot hanging over the fire.

"You eat."

The boys did not know what it was. Charlie took a big spoonful and tasted it. He turned to Joe and said, "This is the best stuff I ever ate. What is it?" The Indian said, "It's venison stew." Charlie swallowed another spoonful. "I have eaten venison stew, but it was never this good."

Lone Eagle went to a box and showed them his herbs. Each kind was wrapped in a piece of cloth and tied into a pouch with a string.

"This what makes taste. Sometime I show you how to make good stew."

Joe said, "This is a good place, Lone Eagle, but why do you live way down here alone?"

The Indian turned dark painful eyes to the boys and said, "I am the only one left now. All the others are dead. Soon I will go, too."

Then Lone Eagle told them the story of the Trail of Tears. "When white man took our lands, we marched west. When we get here we could go no further. Many of our tribe too sick to go on so we stay here, rest go on to Oklahoma. Now all gone except me."

The Indian rose and took their clothes down from the string and gave them to the boys. "They dry. Time to go home before dark."

When they were outside, Lone Eagle went to the back of the shack and came around with two wild turkeys. "You take to mother. No tell about me. You come back, we hunt again."

Mattie could not believe her eyes when the boys showed up at the back door with wild turkeys. "Where on earth have you two been? Charlie, you better run home as quick as you can. Will and John have just left. They have gone to get your father and Jim to go looking for you. We feared the worst when the storm came up."

All that winter they visited Lone Eagle. He always helped them take home plenty of game. Now that it was spring again, the Indian taught them many things, like how to make a whistle out of the green cane that grows along the river banks.

Lone Eagle always knew where the big catfish were hiding, and he helped them to catch a large string of them, every time they visited him. Charlie loved to sit and whittle and listen to the stories Lone Eagle told about the tribe and things he did is a boy.

One day they were in the General Store and they overheard two neighbor women talking about Joe's sister, Mary. Joe was stunned to hear one of them say, "She is breeding by that ole Lafe Dellinger."

Joe ran home so fast, Charlie could not catch him. He burst through the backdoor panting. Mattie caught his shoulder and said,

"Slow down, Joe, what is wrong?"

Joe turned tear-filled eyes to his mother and told her what he had heard in the store. "It's not true, is it, Mama?"

Mattie wiped the flour from her hands and put her arm around the heaving shoulders of her youngest son. "I am afraid it is," she answered.

From that time on, the family could not go anywhere. The talk was so bad, Mary stayed in her room most of the time with the door closed. One night as they sat at supper, the door burst open and Lafe Dellinger walked into the room. The red flash on his face told better than words of his anger.

Will Brawner jumped to his feet and said "What is the meaning of this?"

The lawman turned a dark scowl to Mary and said, "You better quit telling people that I am the father of your brat, or you will be sorry."

Mary stood her ground. "But you know that you are, Lafe, and so does everyone else."

"Just keep your mouth shut, or I'll shut it for you," he ordered. With that warning he went out and slammed the door behind him.

Silence fell on the supper table. Marie turned to her daughter and said, "Maybe we shouldn't say who the father is."

"Mother, he is this child's father, and I am not going to say he is not. He will just have to face up to it."

Late one night in August, Mary's baby was born. It was a

boy. She chose the name Allen for her son. She named him for Charlie's father, whose name was Henry Allen. The family all loved Baby Allen. At most anytime one of them could be found holding him. Next spring he was sitting up and crawling.

That March was stormy. One night they were milking and a severe thunderstorm came up. Will and John finished their cows, but Joe was late. He told him to go to the house to supper, and he would be on as soon as he finished milking and turned the cow out.

It seemed to take him forever. As he stepped inside the screened back porch and set the milk on the table, he heard a loud boom. At first he thought it was thunder, then he heard his mother scream. He crept to the glass pane of the kitchen door and peeped in. What he saw made him shrink back against the wall in terror. Standing inside the dining room, a shotgun in his hands, was Lafe Dellinger.

Will Brawner's headless body slumped forward blood spurting onto the food on the table. Mattie died trying to save baby Allen. The gun barked again and again and bodies felt like trees blown down in a storm, until no one was left alive.

Joe sobbed soundlessly as he saw his entire family wiped out. As he looked into the kitchen, he saw Dellinger going from one body to the other, as if looking for someone.

"My God," thought Joe, "he is counting to see if he got us all." With that thought came terror such as he had never known. He backed into the side room and closed the door. When the lightning flashed again, he saw the ladder leaned up against the trap door that led to the attic.

Almost without thinking he scrambled up the ladder, pushed up the trap door, crawled through, pulling the ladder up after him. The storm was so violent, any noise he made was covered by the loud boom of thunder.

Sobbing softly, he lay still on the trap door. He could hear the deputy going through the house, looking in every room. When When he came into the side room, Joe held his breath. He just knew he could see him in his hiding place.

When the murderer was satisfied that no one else was in the house, he left. Joe heard his horse whinnying as he mounted and passed the side of the house where Joe was hiding.

For a long time, Joe laid perfectly still, praying for his family. He knew without looking that they were all dead. Toward midnight, he finally came down and stepped hesitantly into the kitchen. The lamp still burned on the table.

Blood was all over the table and in the floor. His two sisters fell sideways as they were shot out of their chairs. His mother's body was blown almost in two as she tried to cover the baby.

John had a great gaping hole in his neck, where the blood was clotting now. Joe went to each one and touched them. As he touched his mother's hand, it seemed he could hear her say, "Run, Joe! Save yourself and when the time is right, you can tell who did this to us."

He ran to the cookstove. He took a clean towel and wrapped bread from a pan his mother had not put on the table before the shooting. There was also meat and baked sweet potatoes.

He ran to the bedroom he had shared with John and grabbed a pair of overalls, some underwear, and socks. The clothing, along with the food, he put into a clean flour sack and ran from the house as if demons were after him.

He got as far as the barn and stopped. Where would he go? He knew Lafe Dellinger would hunt him down and kill him, the first opportunity he got. As he stood trembling in the damp night air, a face appeared to him. The dark, pain-filled eyes seemed to beckon him. He knew at once where to go, to Lone Eagle.

He ran, still blubbering to the river where he kept the old boat hidden. With shaking fingers, he untied the rope and jumped in.

The journey through the dark of early morning was one of terror and uncertainty. The first rays of weak sunshine were breaking through the clouds as he pulled the old boat up on the river bank near Lone Eagle's little shack.

As he stumbled through the wet underbrush, he could see smoke coming from the chimney, and he knew Lone Eagle was cooking his breakfast. The door opened, and he could see the Indian standing there with his old rifle in his hands. When he saw Joe, he leaned the gun against the wall and studied the trembling lad with worried eyes. He drew the boy inside and closed the door.

"Some great trouble, or Joe would not be here at this hour."

Joe's legs seem to give way as he clutched Lone Eagle and

began to weep again. The Indian carried him near the fire and wrapped him in a blanket.

"Now you tell Lone Eagle your story." Joe began with Mary giving birth to Allen, then told of the threat Lafe had made. Then Joe told of watching as Lafe murdered his whole family. Joe told Lone Eagle he could not go home, because Lafe would kill him, too, the first chance he got.

The old Indian took the boy's hand and looked deep into his eyes. "You stay here. In a few days we go to place I know, the lawman will help you."

That morning about 8 o'clock, Charlie told his mother he was going to get Joe to go fishing, as it was too wet to work in the fields. As usual he walked up to the back door and pushed it open as he called out, "Joe, where are you?" He called again, but complete silence greeted him.

He took a tentative step into the kitchen. The scene that was before his eyes was one of such a horror that he ran from the house screaming as loudly as he could. Mr. and Mrs. Hawkins were passing by on their way to town. Charlie ran to their wagon as Mr. Hawkins drew the mules to a stop.

He jumped from the wagon and caught Charlie's arm. "What is wrong, son?" Charlie was so shocked that all he could do was point to the Brawner house and say, "They are all dead."

Mr. Hawkins went to look for himself and then told Charlie, "You go get help and send Jim for the sheriff." Soon Sheriff Matheny and his deputy Lafe Dellinger on the scene. The sheriff sent Henry to the casket maker, to order the coffins to bury the family in.

The women of the community washed and laid out Mattie and her two daughters. Two of the men dressed Will and John, as best they could. Will's head was completely off, so they took it and placed it in the casket with his body and closed the lid.

The caskets were lined up around the parlor wall. Lafe Dellinger went through the house, talking to everyone. Charlie stood inside the kitchen listening to him tell everyone that Joe had killed all his family and run away. Charlie could not help wondering where Joe was, but he knew that Joe would never kill anyone.

After the funerals the next day, the ladies the community came in to clean the house and wash everything. Charlie spent the morning keeping the wash pot filled with water and a fire burning around it. At noon time he told his mother he was going down to the river.

He met several men led by Lafe Dellinger as they searched for Joe. "Are you sure you don't know where Joe is hiding?" The deputy asked. "No sir, I don't," Charlie answered.

As Charlie got to the place where they had the old boat hidden and saw that it was gone, joy filled his heart. Now he knew where Joe was.

The next few days talk ran wild around the community. Lafe kept telling everyone that Joe had killed his family. The weekly paper carried the headlines, "Boy Kills Family and Runs

Away."

Every day Charlie worked on a raft he was building. He cut saplings and nailed old boards across them. He made a steering pole out of a long, thin tree limb. When it was ready, he set out early one morning, pushing the raft into the swiftly running water. He used the steering pole to push away from the banks.

As it gliding along, the raft ran under a low hanging branch and a large water moccasin fell near Charlie's foot. He used the pole to knock it back into the river. At last, he came to the place where the boys always left their boat. He pulled the raft out of the river and onto the bank. Lone Eagle's shack was just a short distance into the woods.

A cry of joy greeted Charlie as he came inside of the shack. Joe ran sobbing and threw his arms around him.

Lone Eagle stood in the doorway and watch the two boys. Charlie told them of the happenings of the last few days, and that Lafe was telling everyone that Joe had killed his family.

The two boys were talking about what could be done with Lone Eagle stepped up and said, "We go down river to Linden. Deputy Marshal stay there. Joe tell what he see. Marshal will get that Lafe."

They ate breakfast and left as soon as they could. It was several miles to Linden. Curious stares followed the unlikely looking trio as they inquired where the Marshal could be found.

Soon they were seated in his office inside the jail. Charlie told of the killings of his friend's family and what the deputy was telling everyone about Joe. Joe then told the Marshal the events of a terrible night when he witnessed the slaying of all of his family.

The lawman looked at the old Indian that he had learned to trust when he was a boy. "Is this true, Lone Eagle?"

"Boy tell truth, Marshal."

The Marshal stood from his seat. "You will have to come with me, Joe, so you can tell what you saw." Joe backed away with fear-filled eyes. "No, I can't do that. He will kill me, when he finds out I saw him shoot all of them."

"Well, you go on back with Lone Eagle," Marshal said. "Then you boys make your way on home. I will be there by then, and I will see that no one harms you."

While they were in town, Lone Eagle went to the General Store and bought the supplies he needed. They begged the Indian to go home with them, but he would not.

Charlie's parents, Henry and Dolly, were overjoyed to see Joe, when at nightfall the two boys appeared at their kitchen door. Henry was very angry when Joe told how the deputy had killed all his family. Henry said "Son, no wonder he has hunted you everywhere. Where did you hide?"

Charlie told his father about Lone Eagle and about the hunting. Henry chuckled. "I always thought it strange you boys came back with a load of game every time you went hunting."

As they sat down to supper, Henry told them not to go outside where anyone could see them. When they woke the next morning, Henry had the horses hitched to the wagon and his rifle leaned against the side of the house.

"Come, boys, we are going to town."

Joe said, "Mr. Henry, I am scared to go where Lafe is." Henry put a comforting arm around the boys and said, "I will see to it that he does not hurt you."

A small crowd had gathered in the town square. They hitched the horses to the rail, outside the General Store.

Lafe Dellinger swaggered around the crowd. "When we find that Joe Brawner, we are going to hang him," he boasted.

Joe stared at the big man, hatred blazing from his eyes. He walked up and looked him in the eye and said, "Well, Mr. Deputy Sheriff, here I am." Lafe Dellinger paled as he looked into the hate-filled eyes of the boy. Just as he reached out to grab him, a tall stranger stepped from the crowd.

The stranger's gun was tied low on his hip, and on the front of his vest was a US Marshal's badge. The crowd moved back as the Marshal said, "Mr. Dellinger, you are under arrest for the murder of the Brawner family."

Lafe laughed a high, hysterical laugh. "Now, Marshal, you are not going to believe what some boy tells, are you?" The Marshal turned and with a level stare asked, "Who said anything about a boy?"

Lafe knew he had given himself away, but he continued to bluster all the way to jail.

On the way home, Joe asked Henry to stop and let him go into his house. Henry followed Joe and stopped on the front porch.

"You take as long as you want, Joe. I'll wait here."

Joe walked through the silent rooms. He could almost hear the familiar voices, and when he entered the kitchen, it seemed as if he could see the family sitting down to supper and hear the well-loved voice of his father lifted in a blessing for the food on their table.

With tear-filled eyes, he looked at the table that was a scene of horror the last time he saw it. Now it stood washed clean of all the blood of his beloved family.

The trial lasted only two days. Several witnesses told of the threats Lafe made to Mary. Then Joe took the stand. He told of the horror of the stormy night when all of his family were mercilessly shot as they sat at supper.

The jury was out less than an hour when they came back with a guilty verdict. The judge pronounced the sentence of hanging in two weeks' time.

Every time Joe went to town, he stopped to watch the workmen building the gallows to hang Lafe Dellinger. He felt sorry for Lafe's wife and little girl, but his loss was so great he was consumed by it.

A large crowd gathered to see the hanging. As they lead Lafe onto the platform, a preacher prayed for him. The preacher said, "May God have mercy on your soul." The trap was sprung, and Lafe Dellinger hung, kicking, as Joe turned and walked to the cemetery where his family was buried.

He knelt beside his mother's grave and whispered, "Now

you can rest, Mama. He has paid."

The spring rain fell softly on the fields of newly set tobacco. Joe had stayed each night with Charlie since the hanging. He turned and said, "Mr. Henry, I need someone to help me work the place. What can I do?"

Henry said "Son, why don't you pay a visit to Lone Eagle? He needs someone, too."

That fall, a fine tobacco harvest was gathered, and no one thought it odd that a young boy and an old Indian were considered to have raised the best crop of tobacco in those parts.

(This is a true story that happened in Weakley County, Tennessee in 1906 and 1907. Some of the names have been changed. The young boy named Charlie in the story was the author's father.)

Charlie Myrick Enters the Service

In May 1917, Charlie entered the service in Dresden, Tennessee. He trained at Camp Pike, Arkansas at first, then was sent to Fort Dix, New Jersey for more training. In the spring of 1918, he was sent to Brest, France. The American and French armies were fighting all around Paris. By September, 1918, most of the French towns had been liberated by the advancing armies and the German army had been pushed into the Muse River Valley. The fighting was very fierce, as the unit Charlie was with was moved closer to the front lines. Food was scarce. The mess wagons were not dependable and many times when they reached the troops the bread was molded. Charlie later said, "It wasn't too bad once you pulled all the mold off. And when you were hungry, you didn't care very much how it was, just so it was food." When they were camped near a village, sometimes the farmers would give them food, if the Germans had not taken what they had.

It rained almost every day, the trucks that pulled the mess wagons and cannons were not equipped for all the mud and would stall. They would have to get the French farmers to pull them out with their horses. Charlie recalled a night when they had not had any food all day. One of the men, a private, 'Blackie' as his friends called him, was from around Enterprise, near where Charlie eventually lived in Mississippi. He asked all his buddies to give him what few coins they had, and he went into the village and found a card game. He came back some hours later, with a large rooster and a small pig, which they cooked. Charlie said it tasted pretty good to the hungry soldiers.

At the end of October 1918, word came that the end of the war was near. The Captain told Charlie that he would be running the mail and messages to the front lines. This was a very dangerous job, as they had to run through some of the fiercest fighting. Everyone that had the job before Charlie had been killed.

In the evening after a big battle, Charlie was sent on a night run to the front lines. Just before he started out a thunderstorm came up. He had to run through the battlefield where the fighting had taken place that day. As he was running, he stepped on something and almost fell. When the lightning flashed, he could see what he had tripped on clearly. He was looking into the eyes of a dead German soldier while standing on the man's stomach. Charlie had nightmares about that the rest of his days.

On the 10th of November, Charlie was sent to the front lines with messages for his Captain. He put on his gas mask and started out. The Germans had sprayed the battlefield with mustard gas. Without a gas mask, one did not live long. The German army was retreating, and as Charlie got closer to the front lines, he noticed a pair of Clydesdale horses, that the Germans had used to pull cannons across the battlefield. They were standing in their 'traces', heads lowered, swaying from side to side. Charlie noticed they did not have gas masks on. Being a horse lover, Charlie went over to speak a word of comfort to them. Just before he got there, a sniper's bullet went down his rib cage, piercing his gas mask, letting the poison gas into his lungs. The last thing he remembered was seeing the Clydesdales fall to the ground. The weight of the great beasts shook the ground under his feet, he lost consciousness, and fell beside them.

When he woke, he was in a field hospital with his lungs burning like fire. Every breath he took was torture because the gas destroyed the lung's filtering system. The next morning around 11 o'clock, word came that the war was over, "Armistice had been signed!" The next day, Charlie was transferred to a hospital where his adventure had begun, in Brest, France. Catholic nuns, who were very good to the Americans that had helped to liberate their country, ran the hospital. With the harbors opened up, several Dutch ships brought food and medicine into France, which meant at last they had enough food to feed the soldiers.

While Charlie was in the hospital, the French Government brought him a medal, which was the equivalent of the American Purple Heart. He stayed in the French hospital until March 1919 at which time they put him on the ship 'Leviathan' and sent him home. The crossing home was good for Charlie, the salty air helped clear his lungs of the poison. When they docked in Hoboken, New Jersey, he was sent to the V.A. Hospital in Alexandria, Louisiana. It was there he was diagnosed with Tuberculosis.

Not much was known then about chemical poisoning. Not until 1953, did a doctor admit that Charlie had chemical poisoning from the German's mustard gas. The doctor at the V.A. Hospital in Memphis, said after looking at his x-rays, "Mr. Myrick, you clearly have Mustard Gas Poisoning."

"Thank you, we have waited a long time to hear a Doctor say that." Charlie replied.

Nearly 60 years later, Charlie was awarded the Purple Heart from the American Government.

He passed away June 30, 1983

Note: The author's son, Tony Gates, has done extensive genealogy research and came across an interesting tidbit. Listed on the crew manifest for Charlie's trip home aboard the Leviathan, was one young Humphrey Bogart.

The Country Doctor

(This story is copyrighted by The University of Mississippi and is reprinted here with permission.)

The heat rose in a shimmering haze across the fields, the rows of cotton that had to be hoed seemed endless, each one of us put our backs to the task before us.

As I neared the end of my row I saw a cloud of dust rising as if someone came down the road at a fast pace. I bent to get the water jug sitting under a bush, the car came to a stop and I saw it was Dr. Windham; he leaned out the window and said, "You kids get the seine out and get me some crayfish. I'll be back in a little while. I'm on my way to the Billings. Their boy Dean is sick."

Tommy and I went to the small stream near the cotton

patch and seined out the doctor a half bushel of crayfish, we put them in the wash tub to wait for him to come back along.

It was near sundown when he finally came, Mama was coming from the barn, two buckets brimming with milk. She came to stand near where we were putting the crayfish into a bucket for the doctor to take home with him.

He raised his head and looked Mama in the eye and said, "Well you take good care of these kids, I have just come from the Billings and their boy, Dean, is really sick. I don't know what is wrong, but I believe it is infantile paralysis, like President Roosevelt had."

Dr. James H. Windham was the only doctor close to our home. His office was in Ecru. His word was law as far as we were concerned. When Mama asked him what caused this disease and what she should do to keep us from having it, I knew she was really scared.

He appeared to study the ground for an answer. He finally said, "Lela, if we only knew what caused it, maybe we could do something to stop it."

Mama seemed resigned to the fact that she could do nothing about that, so she said to the doctor, "Do you want me to fix your crayfish for you? We can put them in the wash pot and boil them." He said "Well, I would do that, but Monty said she would cut the tails off for me while I make some more calls. Then we will make gumbo out of them."

After the doctor left I asked Mama how he could eat those

nasty crayfish and she just smiled and said, "When the tails are cut off and the shell is removed there is a piece of tender white meat inside." I did not think I would want any of it.

Time passed slowly, every day we would see the doctor's car by, going to see Dean. Everyone thought Dean would die. No one went to visit. They did not know if the germ would be taken back to their children, so they stayed away.

Every time the doctor came by, he told of another case of the paralysis. Several children died from it, others like Dean Billings were crippled for life.

One day the doctor stopped and said, "Charlie, you come go with me to the office I have fixed up some medicine for you to use on the children." That night after we had our baths, Daddy lined us up and filled the strange looking bottle with the red medicine. It had a long stem with a rubber squeeze pump on one end of it. We had to open our mouths as wide as we could and Daddy sprayed the red medicine into our throats. This was supposed to keep us from having "infantile paralysis". That is what they called Polio in 1939.

One morning about daylight, Dr. Windham came by and stopped. I went to the door. He looked so tired, but the twinkle was still in his eye as he said, "Good morning, Curly Top. What is wrong with you, fever and lurk. Two stomachs to eat and none to work!" That little rhyme of his always made me laugh. I said, Come in Doctor, we were just about to eat breakfast." He turned to Mama and said, "I stopped to see if I could get a bite to eat."

Mama had cut the last ham of the season the day before. She had coffee boiling, and biscuits baking. The doctor came in to the kitchen and sat at the table after he had washed his hands on the back porch. Daddy came from the barn, washed his hands, and sat down to eat.

"What brings you out this early, Doc?"

"I have been delivering a baby over at the Kidd's. Since I had some more calls to make down this way, I thought I would stay while I was here."

Mama asked how the children were doing that had paralysis and he looked up at her as she filled his cup with coffee. "Lela, I am just an old country doctor. What do I know? When I see these people suffering and dying and I don't know what to do for them. I think of what the prophet Jeremiah said in chapter 8 verse 21 through 22, "I weep for the heart of my people, I stand amazed, dumb with grief, is there no medicine in Gilead? Is there no physician? Why doesn't God do something? Why doesn't he help?"

Mama patted him on the shoulder, "We think you know as much as any city doctor and you are our friend. You care what happens to us." He seemed to feel a bit better when Mama told him that. The twinkle was back in his eye as he told Mama, "No one can make biscuits like you, Lela. That's why I always stop and bum a breakfast off you when I'm in this neighborhood."

After we finished eating the doctor left to make his rounds in the neighborhood, he always stopped at each house whether he was sent for or not.

Like all bad things, the Polio epidemic came and went, leaving those that lost little ones forever grieving for them. The crippled, such as Dean Billings, having to adjust to a new way of life.

Many years passed with Dr. Windham still making his calls on his beloved patients, stopping to see his many friends. When he died at an old age, I went to the funeral home. As I looked down at the snow-white hair and slight figure, many memories came back to me. I could see myself at four when I stepped on a needle. It stuck in the ball of my foot. There were no x-rays at the time, so Dr. Windham had to peel the skin off the bottom of my foot and probe for the needle. I could see him as he said to me, "Now Curly Top, this is going to hurt, but if you will be a big girl and not cry, when we are through we will go get an ice cream cone."

I remembered when a friend drowned, how we came down to the river. When the body was recovered, he worked tirelessly trying to revive her—knowing all the time it was useless. And when he could do no more, he stayed all day with the family, trying to comfort them.

I thought about how his life and been intertwined with ours since the day we were delivered and how I had loved him all my life. I turn to some friends with tears in my eyes and said, "These doctors we have now, they may have more to work with and they may have better ways to help us, but when all men like Dr. Windham are gone, the heart of medicine will be gone, too."

Harvest of Love

The old man and the child stood on the windswept hilltop looking across the brown earth in the small valley below. The child snuggled closer in her worn sweater and cap. The old man looked down at the shivering child and with merry blue eyes asked, "Child, do you see them big watermelons?"

The child said, "No, Pappy, I don't see them."

"Well, come August you will," he replied.

He took her hand and started back down the hill. As he slowly walked, the child skipped around him chattering, "How many melons will we have this year, Pappy?"

When they walked into the warm kitchen where Lela was preparing dinner, she looked up at them. "What have you two been doing?"

Elizabeth answered her mother, "Pappy says we are going to have lots of melons come August, and I am going to help plant them this year."

Lela looked at the old man, who was well into his 80s now. "Pappy, you know you don't need to be planting such a big patch of melons this year. At your age you are not able to work them."

He patted his daughter-in-law's hand. "Well, I've got me a good hand this year. I 'spect she will be doing all the hard work."

Lela just shook her head and laughed. "Well, I see you have your plans made, and it's just the first of March. We will be having cold weather coming along before we think of planting anything."

Lela set the table for dinner and told the family to wash their hands. The hot vegetable soup was so good they all had second helpings.

When they had finished eating, the old man placed the checkerboard on the table. "Want to play a game, child?" he asked. Elizabeth was always happy to spend time with her grandfather. Henry Allen Myrick was a tall, sparse man with twinkling blue eyes and lots of snow-white curly hair.

Born before the Civil War, he had many memories of bad times and trouble, but to look at his serene and pleasant face, you would never know he had a care in the world.

His wife, Dolly, was entirely different, always grumbling about something or sick abed. No one in the family cared for her, they only tolerated her because they loved him.

Henry and Dolly had lived with their son and his family for years. Henry was always pleasant and loving to the children and Lela, but Dolly was like a child herself, always finding fault with everything and everyone. She was especially critical of Lela. No matter how hard she tried, Lela could never please Dolly

In the following weeks it was stormy and cold. The rain came down in endless torrents. Elizabeth stood by the window one day holding her doll, looking out at the gray rainy sky. Henry sat in the cane bottomed settee reading his Bible. Elizabeth walked over to him and said, "Pappy, if it keeps raining will we need an ark?"

The old man looked startled at the question and turned to the wide-eyed child with a smile. "Well no, child, I don't think we will. Why, before long the sun will be shining and the purple daisies will be up all over the pasture, and Bess and Star can eat their fill. Then we will have 'Daisy Milk' to drink."

He held out his arms. "Come, child, and I will sing to you." Elizabeth climbed into his lap and snuggled her head on his shoulder as he began to sing in his pure Irish tenor voice.

>   *Green coffee grows on a white oak tree*
>   *The river flows with Brandy-O*
>   *Go choose the one to walk with you*
>   *He's sweet as striped candy-O*

The singing continued with 'The Turkish Lady,' then 'Greensleeves.' Elizabeth's eyes grew heavy and soon she was sound asleep.

The next few weeks brought warmer weather. With the sunshine and wind, the earth dried enough for Henry's son Charlie to plow the small valley.

He hitched Prince, the big red Belgian horse, to the breaking plow. Henry watched as the earth broke open beneath the sharp point of the plow. When Charlie had plowed the ground, he took the harrow and, with its sharp iron teeth, broke all the clods until the ground was smooth and ready for planting.

Charlie then hitched Prince to the slide and hauled several loads of barnyard fertilizer and dumped it beside the patch Henry used for his melons.

Every day Henry and Elizabeth walked to the patch to inspect it. Henry got down and felt the soil to see how warm it was. It had to be just right, or the melon seeds would not sprout.

On the day it was ready, he took his little thin hoe and made hills for each melon. Elizabeth had a small bucket in which she brought the fertilizer to her grandfather. Each hill got a bucket of the right black fertilizer. Henry said barnyard was the best for growing melons.

Now that the seeds were in the ground the old man and the child went every day to see that no weeds came up in the patch. After the planting, Henry would not allow anyone back in the patch with horse and plow. He did all the tilling with his little hoe.

Charlie had made Elizabeth a small table and a wooden bench to sit on. Henry had an old cane-bottom chair that he kept in the tobacco barn. They placed these in the shade of the giant oaks that surrounded the tobacco barn, at the end of the melon patch. They spent many hours just sitting and talking in the cool shade.

As the fledgling plants began to show through the earth, Henry taught Elizabeth how do be sure it lay just right as it began to run along the ground. Each day they inspected the patch for weeds and grass. Elizabeth had a small hoe. She worked the middles and Henry hoed around the young plants.

In early June, the first melons appeared on the vines. Henry turned them every day to be sure they were not one-sided and would be perfectly round. He told Elizabeth that they would have to make sure the chickens did not come that far up the hill and peck holes in the young melons.

Whitey, the old one-eyed gander, strutted around the barnyard. Every time Elizabeth came near, he started toward her with wings dragging the ground, hissing. He always wanted to fight something. He had lost one eye in a fight with the turkey gobbler.

Dick, the hired hand, was cleaning the barn one day when he killed a large chicken snake. He was bringing it to show to Henry and Elizabeth when Whitey spotted Elizabeth running toward Dick. Down with the wings and the hissing started.

Dick called, "Wait, Elizabeth, I'll fix him." He grabbed a piece of rope and tied around the snake's head and as Whitey was getting ready to attack Elizabeth, Dick threw the looped end of the rope around Whitey's neck. The old gander looked back and when he saw the snake, he hopped and jumped trying to get away from it. When he could not, he started honking and took to the air. He looked back and the snake was still with him, and he fell to the ground in a dead faint.

Elizabeth patted her hands with glee, and Henry laughed until the tears ran down his seamed face. Dick walked over and took the snake loose from the old gander, who was still out cold. Henry finally managed to stop laughing long enough to say, "Well, Dick, I hope that old gander has finally learned his lesson."

The crops were all in and growing. Every morning before the dew was off the plants, Henry took the children to the tobacco patch to pick the huge green worms off the leaves. Charlie always built a small fire at the end of the rows, and when they had a picked a large amount of the worms they took them and threw them into the fire.

There was no poison, so that was the only way to control the pests. Elizabeth hated the worms. She was afraid of them, and every day she would cry when she had to help pick them from the tobacco leaves. She woke at night screaming in terror because she dreamed the worms were crawling all over her. Finally, Lela gave her an old pair of blunt-tip scissors to kill them with so she wouldn't have to touch them.

The vegetables had to be picked and shelled so Lela could can them. The long rows of butter beans and peas were good hiding places for snakes, so the children always called the two spotted feists, Roosevelt and Hoover, to go to the garden with them. One day Elizabeth bent toward a pea vine, when Roosevelt ran in between her and the vine. She jumped back and he pulled out a big copperhead, shaking it until it was dead.

Elizabeth, along with her sister Faye and her brother Thomas, played on Sunday afternoons after church in the white sand that was the path between the house and the barn. They made frog houses by placing their bare feet flat on the ground and packing dirt tight around them until they could pull them out and leave a small dirt house. They caught frogs and put them into the houses and put sticks across the opening to keep them from escaping.

The summer heat was intense. Henry and Elizabeth went every day to the melon patch. They hoed around the melons and pulled weeds from around the plants where they ran along the ground. The rain and heat made the vines grow at a rapid rate. The melons were as big as buckets by the end of July.

One day after weeding the patch, Elizabeth pulled off her top shirt and hung it on a limb to dry. Henry came to the shade under the big oak trees near the patch. Elizabeth ran to get his chair so he could sit and rest.

His worn blue jumper was wet, and Elizabeth asked, "Pappy, why do you wear a coat and it's so hot?"

He eased into the chair and said, "Child, anything that will keep out the cold will also keep out the heat."

They sat and talked. Henry told her about the time Grant's army crossed the river near their house on its way to Shiloh. He was a lad of nine that April morning of 1862 when he stood hidden in some bushes on the banks of the river and watched as they made log barges to float their cannons and horses across the river.

He told of how scared he was when the Union soldiers went to their house and split all their featherbeds open looking for valuables. When they found nothing, they held them up and watched as the wind blew all the feathers away.

He told how they took all their food and left him nothing to eat. He watched as they carried off all the chickens and hogs they could catch, thrown across the saddles of the big red horses they rode.

Elizabeth could listen all day, as he told how his father Moses buried the gristmill engine beneath the hog pen so the Yankees could not find it. They would look in every place that was freshly dug, but they never thought to dig beneath the mud of the hog pen.

The old man's mind was sharp and clear as he painted word pictures of the battlefield after the battle. Elizabeth never forgot the pain she saw in his eyes as he told of the suffering of the people that lost everything they had because of the war.

The old man and the child would sit for hours in the cool shade. Sometimes he would drift off to sleep with his chair propped against the tobacco barn with his head resting on the rough planks. What he did, Elizabeth would sit quietly and sing in her little girl voice until he woke.

That August they had a different preacher for the protracted meeting at the Baptist Church. He talked most of the time in a calm moderate voice. Suddenly he would holler as loud as he could, "Oh God!" and scare everyone.

One night, Lela had spread a quilt in the corner of the church as was the custom, and Thomas and Elizabeth laid down with several other small children and went to sleep.

As the sermon progressed all the children were asleep on the pallet except Ben Conolly, who lay on the bench next to where his mother was sitting. As the preacher talked, Ben slowly drifted into a fitful sleep. Suddenly the preacher hollered, "Oh, God!" And Ben jumped and rolled off the bench, catching his neck on the two pieces of wood at the bottom of the bench. He started screaming as loud as he could and woke up all the other children, who started crying. It broke up the meeting for that night.

Early one morning Henry called Elizabeth and said, "Come, child, it's time to sample our melons."

He took two knives in the salt shaker, a bucket with water in it and a rag, and they walked up the hill to the melon patch.

The dew glistened on the green skins of the melons. Henry took the wet rag and wiped the table. He then went to the patch and selected a melon. He brought it to the table. Elizabeth could hardly wait as he split the melon open.

Henry sat at the small table and began to cut into the melon. He cut the middle out of one half and handed it to

Elizabeth. "Here, child, take the heart. It is the best part."

Elizabeth held the melon in both hands and began to eat. The juice ran down her small chin and dripped onto the ground.

Henry laughed as he said, "Don't gobble it up so fast, child. There is plenty."

The cool fresh melon was so good it was hard to eat slowly.

When they had eaten their fill, Elizabeth asked, "Pappy, what will we do with all these melons?"

The old man said, "We will share them with our friends and neighbors. Dr. Windham will be coming along soon, and we will pull a nice, big one for him."

The old man went into the shed beside the tobacco barn and brought out the wheelbarrow. "Come, child, and we will gather the melons that are ready before the sun heats them up."

Together they went from one vine to another. Henry would decide which ones were ready.

"Pappy, how do you know which one is ripe?"

He showed her the small twig that fastened the melon to the vine. "See this child? When it is brown, the melon is ripe."

They gathered a wheelbarrow full and placed them inside the tobacco barn where it was cool. The barn was empty as it was not time to harvest the tobacco.

Henry took off his worn black hat and fanned himself with the brim. Elizabeth said, "Pappy, why don't you let me put the wheelbarrow up and you sit down and rest a while." She could see he was worn out.

"Don't mind if I do, child," he answered as he leaned back and closed his eyes.

One day, Dr. Windham came along and stopped to visit for a few minutes. Henry had brought one of his largest melons and had it cooling in the well house. He brought it around to the front porch and said, "Doc, I want to give you one of my melons."

The doctor looked the old man up and down, then asked, "How old are you now, Mr. Henry?"

"Eighty-four," Henry answered.

"I have told you time and again you are going to fall dead in that hot sun."

"Well, I'd just as soon die in my melon patch as anywhere, Doc."

The doctor took Elizabeth's hand and said, "Miss Curly, I am going to turn this patient over to you. Now don't you let him out in the sun except early in the morning and late in the afternoon."

The harvest was upon them. The tobacco had to be cut and hung in the barn to dry, the cotton picked, and the corn and soybeans gathered. Henry worked in the field along with the children until Charlie would tell Elizabeth, "Take your grandfather to the shade."

That winter Elizabeth started to school. She was so excited to be going. Charlie bought her a lunchbox with circus horses on it.

One afternoon she sat with tablet and pencil writing the alphabet. Henry walked by the table and stopped to tousle her curly mop of straw-colored hair.

"What are you going to be when you grow up, child?" He asked.

With serious round eyes Elizabeth answered, "I am going to write stories about the things you have told me."

Henry laughed. "Well, as good as you like to eat, you better find something else to do, child, or you will go hungry. Because no one would care what I have to say."

"I would," she answered, "and I bet a lot of other people will, too."

Henry's birthday was coming up on the 12th of November. Lela baked a birthday cake with the white icing he loved. The icing was made with water and sugar cooked into a stiff syrup and beaten into egg whites.

The older girls helped him dress in his Sunday suit and tie for the party. Lela cooked a guinea hen and made dressing because it was Henry's favorite food.

All the children gathered around him as he cut his cake and he gave each one a piece. Elizabeth thought how handsome he looked in his dark blue serge suit and white shirt, with his freshly shampooed silvery hair shining in the lamp light.

All that winter and into Spring Henry's steps became slower. He tired easily, and when he sat down he was most often asleep.

On a warm day in late April, Lela was dressing a chicken to fry. Henry came into the backyard where she was picking off the feathers. He was carrying his fishing pole.

"Lela, put the chicken entrails in a can for me. I'm going fishing."

Lela looked at her father-in-law. "I'd rather you didn't go by yourself, Pappy. Let Elizabeth go with you."

"I am going to the river run. Can she walk that far?"

"I think she can," Lela answered.

Lela called to Elizabeth. "Come go with Pappy fishing and put some shoes on your feet."

The old man and the child walked down the road until they could cut across the fields to make it closer to the river.

Henry baited the hooks and set several poles in the side of the bank. They found a fallen tree to sit on near the water's edge and held their hooks in the water.

The mosquitoes skipped across the surface of the water and in the still warm sun Elizabeth was almost asleep when her pole was jerked so hard she almost lost it.

"Pappy," she yelled, "I think I have a big one!"

The old man rose slowly and helped her pull the pole out of the bank. He took the big catfish off the hook and put it on a stringer and tied it to a willow bush.

In the next hour they took three off the hooks that were set, and then Henry caught a large one. Elizabeth was scared when he almost fell in the water, and she was glad when he said it was time to go home.

A few nights later it was so warm Henry and Elizabeth

were sitting in the swing on the front porch. They were facing the east, as the moon rose, full and round, over the treetops, Elizabeth laid her head against her grandfather's shoulder.

"Sing to me, Pappy."

He put his arm around her and began to sing softly.

Suddenly he stopped. "Set up, babe, we must get your mother and get to the cellar. It's going to storm."

"Why do you say that, Pappy? I can see the moon."

Henry pointed toward the moon. "See that dark cloud rising up under the moon? Always remember, child, when you see a dark cloud rising up under a full moon it will be a bad storm, now run and get your mama."

By the time they all got coats and Lela lit the lantern and got everyone into the cellar it was hailing so hard it sounded like bullets hitting the tin roof of the cellar.

When the storm was over the ground was so covered with hail stones they could hardly walk over them. Thomas asked Lela if they could make ice cream now that they had some ice.

Lela made up the custard while the children gathered buckets of the ice, and they all enjoyed a bowl of ice cream before bedtime.

The melon patch was planted once more, and Henry and Elizabeth worked it with the hoes. Elizabeth tried to do most of the work. She was seven now and could see that Henry was not as strong as he had been in the past two summers.

He sat in his old cane-bottomed chair leaned back against

the tobacco barn, eyes closed. Elizabeth took the top off the water jug and asked, "Pappy, do you want a drink of water?"

The old man opened his eyes and with a faraway look said, "Child, I was dreaming of my homeland."

"Where is that?" she inquired.

"Ireland," he answered. "Always remember that is where we came from," and the child said, "Yes, I will remember."

The melons were harvested, and the hot sun glistened on the still surface of the river where Henry love to sit and fish. His steps were even slower now, and Elizabeth always went along to watch after him.

In the still twilight Henry sat and sang Elizabeth to sleep every night, even though Lela would gently remind her that she was such a big girl now her feet touched the floor when she sat in Henry's lap.

That October the pumpkins were very large, and at Halloween Charlie carved faces on several, and the children lit candles inside them. Henry laughed and told Elizabeth to set them on the porch to ward off the goblins that might be coming by.

The first of November turned cold and every morning the frost was thick on the windowpanes. During the second week of the month Henry could not get up one morning. When Lela went to see about him the first thing she noticed was the red spots on his cheeks, and when she felt his brow it burned her hand.

She called Charlie and told him to go for the doctor at once. When Dr. Windham arrived and examined him, he came into the kitchen where Lela was putting breakfast on the table.

He said, "Mr. Henry has pneumonia and at his age, he may not make it."

Elizabeth hid behind the door of the bedroom and cried until her eyes were swollen shut. All the neighbors took turns sitting up with Henry, but as the days wore on he became worse. On the 18th of November, he quietly slipped away.

Nearly sixty years later Elizabeth returned to the hillside. She stood under the ancient oaks and looked over the small valley.

She closed her eyes, and in the sighing wind in the tall trees she seemed to hear a pure Irish tenor voice singing about white oak trees that could grow green coffee and a river that could flow with brandy.

And in the early morning sunshine she could see fat green melons ready for harvest and an old man and a young child sitting in the cool shade enjoying the fruits of their labor.

And she knew that not only was there a harvest of melons, but one of love.

Daddy's Love Gave Me Strength in Hard Times

My Christmas memory goes back to a few days before Christmas in the mid-1930s.

The day started cold and cloudy with a mist of snow blowing from the north. My mother was cooking breakfast as Daddy came in from the barn. They whispered together as Daddy washed his hands and sat down to eat.

Mother got his coat, scarf, and hat and brought them to warm by the black iron stove. I knew that meant Daddy was going to town. We lived about 14 miles from New Albany, and at that time there were only a few cars in the community. The Depression had taken its toll on all of us. I knew if someone did not come along that knew him and give him a ride, he would have to walk all the way. But he started out, confident someone would be going to town and offer him a ride.

All day while Mama baked cakes and pies for Christmas, my brother and sisters and I worked to decorate the house. My two older sisters hung up the red and green roping across the dining room and hung the red paper bell in the middle. My brother and I strung red holly berries and made red and green paper chains out of old wrapping paper Mama had saved.

All day the sky grew darker and the wind rose higher. I saw Mama looking out the window several times and I knew she was worried about Daddy out in the cold. I heard her say to Ruth, my oldest sister, "I sure hope your daddy gets back before it starts to snow."

We fed the animals early and got in wood and water for the night. It was my job to fill the lamps with oil and wash the chimneys. When all our work was done for the day and Mama was cooking supper, I stood by the window watching for Daddy.

It had been snowing hard for the last hour or more, when just before dark, I saw someone coming up the road. Sure enough, it was Daddy, but he seemed to be having trouble walking in the deepening snow. I saw he was carrying a large, heavy-looking sack over his shoulder. When I told Mama about the sack, she said it was feed for the cows.

Mama got the washbasin and filled it with warm water and set it by the stove. When Daddy came in the house, he was almost frozen. Mama helped him take off his wet coat. My brother and I untied his shoes so he could soak his feet in the pan of warm water. Mama asked if he had to walk all the way and he said he got a ride most of the way there, but had to walk from the highway coming back, which was over 5 miles. As soon as he ate his supper, he went to bed. On Christmas morning, we were so happy with what Santa had brought, I forgot about Daddy's trip to town.

Many years later, as I was up almost all night every night caring for Daddy as he was dying from cancer, sometimes I felt that my back would break. But just when I felt that I could not bend another time, my memory went back to that cold afternoon so many years before and I could see a young man walking down a snowy country road, his back bent under a heavy sack of what I realized later in life was our Christmas presents.

He loved us enough to walk miles in the snow so Santa could visit us Christmas morning. When I remembered that, it was not nearly so hard to bend my back again.

Son of the Heart

Lela sat by the dying fire, patting the backside of the wailing infant. The old cane-bottomed rocker creaked as she rocked and patted, trying desperately to quiet the cold. It seemed that none of the remedies for colic worked with this one, born on the fourteenth day of the new year of nineteen thirty-two. The child had cried all night every night. Finally, with a shuddering sigh, the infant drifted into a fitful sleep.

Lela eased the sleeping child into the warm brick-lined basket and started to lie down in her own warm bed, hoping that she could catch a quick nap before time for the new day to begin. Just before she had time to straighten out here tired body under the covers, she heard the sound again. It had been snowing for the last three hours and the wind whistling around the corners of the old house sounded like a lost soul moaning. She swung her feet to the cold floor and shuffled the few steps to the window to peek out beyond the front porch.

What she saw made her forget the chance of a nap. She cried out, "Charlie, get up quick! Someone is lying on the ground outside and there is blood all over the snow!"

Jumping from bed, Charlie grabbed a heavy coat hanging on a nail beside the door to cover his long underwear which he slept in during the winter months. He then slid his feet into his worn plow shoes and clumsily made for the door.

Since he had been elected Justice of the Peace of their small community, he had been involved in almost anything one could think of—from settling disputes between his neighbors, to thieves snatching chickens or running moonshine. The depression had made some new strange bedfellows in this part of the country. As he stared down at the pitiful figure lying in the snow, Lela crept up behind him with the lamp held close. Charlie turned the body over so they could see his face.

"Why, he's just a boy," Charlie exclaimed, "and look how he's been beaten." The two of them half dragged, half carried him into the house. While Charlie stirred up the fire, Lela got some rags and warm water from the black kettle she always kept on the hearth.

The boy was numb with cold and his hands were blue. HIs clothes were wet as if he had been lying there for a long time in the icy snow. Lela tried to pick the pieces of his blue work shirt out of the deep gashes on his back. As she bathed his torn flesh, it was all she could do to not be sick. What kind of monster could inflict such a beating on a child... and why?

The boy shook and whimpered as Lela put salve and homemade bandages on his deep wounds. The boy's eyes were glazed with pain and shock and a sob escaped his lips although he tried desperately to bite it back. Charlie laid a comforting hand on the boy's shoulder, "Now son, can you tell us what happened and who you are?"

The child gulped a few times and finally answered, "My name is Richard Rush. We live across the woods. We moved into the old Hardin place this fall. After Christmas we all came down with the measles and flu. Mother and my little sister both died. Daddy just got meaner and meaner and nothin' I did pleased him. Tonight, he told me to feed the mules and I did like he said; he was drinking and he went out to the barn, and when he came back to the house he said I threw the mules' corn into the mud. He had a piece of chain in his hand and when I told him I hadn't done it, he started to beat me. After I came to, a while later, I remembered that he neighbors had told me about you being the law and if I'd ever needed, you could help. So, I started across the woods, and when I couldn't run, I crawled. That's why my clothes is so wet."

Lela asked the boy if he could sleep some, if she fixed him a bed. "Yessum, I guess I could if I can lay my head down," he told her. She handed him a worn night shirt and led him to the room where her small son, Tommy, was sleeping. "Put this on," she explained, "and give me your wet clothes so I can hang them by the fire to dry."

She waited just outside the door and shortly he handed her his soaked overalls. She heard him lie down beside Tommy, so she tiptoed over and tucked the quilts around the boy and he snuggled down into the warmth of the shared bed. As she turned to leave the room, the boy gently grabbed her hand. "Miss Lela, I sure do thank you for what you did for me. And I'll try to pay you back some day. Honest, I will." She patted his small work-roughened hand and smoothed the dark matted hair from his face, her heart overcome with compassion. "Don't you worry, Richard, you just try to rest now. You are safe here."

Charlie was pacing back and forth as Lela came back into the room to hang the boy's sodden clothes to dry by the fire. When she'd finished, they laid down, both exhausted trying to decide what to do about the boy. They talked in hushed voices until light flooded the room and another new day began.

Lela rose, stoked the fire, and took a shovel-full of coals to the black cook stove in the kitchen. As she prepared breakfast, Charlie went to the barn to feed the animals. Lela got the older children up and ready for school. The covered wagon that came by for them was soon creaking down the road, the big red horses breaking ice each time they put a heavy foot down. The children's eyes were round with curiosity about the unknown boy asleep in little Tommy's bed. Lela handed each of them a small bucket with their lunch tucked inside and hurried them out to the school wagon.

When she returned to the kitchen to fix Charlie's breakfast, the boy was up and dressed in his torn shirt and overalls. He was standing by the stove staring longingly at the meat and biscuits. Charlie stepped inside, smiled at the boy and showed him where to wash his hands and face. Lela sat two plates on the table and motioned for the boy to sit and eat with Charlie.

As Lela passed behind the boy in his chair, she noticed blood oozing through the bandages she had applied hours before. "Charlie, we're going to have to call the doctor and have him take a look at Richard's back. I don't want blood poisonin' to set up from that rusty chain."

The boy was clearly frightened at this and started to cry once more. Lela comforted him, "Don't be afraid, son, no one is going to hurt you anymore."

Charlie changed his clothes and got out the A-Model car. On the way into town, Charlie spoke to the boy about anything he could think of, hoping to take Richard's mind off the place they were headed because it was clear the boy was scared.

Dr. Windham was a medium-sized, wiry man with twinkling blue eyes. Those eyes and his tart manner put his patients as ease. He could be as gentle as a mother, yet he could also be as mean as a grizzly bear when he saw an act of injustice. Dr. Windham was never afraid to tell anyone just what he thought. He took one look at Richard's back and turned angrily to Charlie, "Good God Almighty! Who in thunder action did this to this child?"

Before Charlie could answer, Richard spoke up. "My father did, sir." Dr. Windham was surprised by the boy's casual acceptance of the beating. It was all the good doctor could do to not mutter some things that would have been most unbecoming of his profession.

The doctor questioned the boy about what he was going to do. Richard started to cry and became so upset the doctor said, "You are not going back to that father of yours; the next time he will most likely kill you, son."

As it happened, the doctor had a son who was a lawyer in the next town. Dr. Windham made a phone call asking his son to fix up papers to keep the boy's father away from him. Dr. Windham was still angry as he turned, saying, "Now Charlie, you are the law in that community. What are you going to do with this boy?"

Charlie went to open this mouth, but the words came from the boy, "I would like to stay with Mr. Charlie and Miss Lela. That is... if Mr. Charlie will let me."

The doctor pulled a thunderstruck expression, "Tarnation, boy, he's got five youngins of his own. He don't need another mouth to feed and it being the middle of a depression."

Richard's thin shoulders drooped as he hung his head in despair. "Well, I guess I'll have to go back home then, because there is nowhere else I can go."

Tears came to Charlie's eyes as the scene from the night

before replayed in his mind. "No," Charlie quipped, "No, you will not, son, you will come live with us." Richard's face brightened upon hearing this news, but Charlie raised a hand to him, "I can't pay you any wages, but you will have enough to eat and as many clothes as my own children and always a clean bed to sleep in at night."

So, Richard came home to the old farm house, welcomed by all of Charlie and Lela's family who accepted him as if he'd always been there. Richard helped Charlie with the farm work and all the chores around the farm. Lela never had to tell him to bring in water or wood for the cook stove or fireplace. He seemed to always know what needed done and made sure it was done in a timely fashion.

On one particular night, when the infant had cried all day and Lela was still up rocking at midnight, she turned to see Richard quietly enter the room. He cautiously came to her and stood looking down at the fussy child. "Let me rock her a while, Miss Lela. I know you're plum give out." Lela rose to her achy feet and placed the baby in his arms. Richard sweetly laid her across his shoulder and began rhythmically patting and rocking. Lela thought she would just lie down and rest for just a moment. The creaking of the old rocker soon put her into a deep sleep.

The crowing of the rooster entered Lela's tired mind as she swam up through the warm maze of consciousness. With a jolt, she jumped from the bed and flew into the room where she had left Richard rocking the baby. What she saw made her tiptoe the last few steps, for he was sitting right where she had left him, the infant's face buried in his neck, both his arms wrapped around her. Both were fast asleep.

Spring came that year with high winds in March and violent thunderstorms. Richard and Charlie cleaned out the horse stables and hauled the manure to the fields. They plowed and harried it under in preparation for planting. Charlie sat on the mule-drawn cultivator watching the boy hook up a team of young horses. Since he had lost some of the fear of his father, he was like a young colt himself. With the good wholesome food Lela cooked each day, the boy had also lost that drawn worried look and was starting to fill out. It seemed to Charlie that the child had grown several inches in the last few weeks. It was easy to see the boy would be a big tall man when he reached his full potential.

With the coming of warm weather, Charlie always insisted that the children have Typhoid shots since every summer there was an outbreak of the dreaded fever. The older girls, Ruth, Pearl, and Faye started to cry as soon as Lela told them the day had come to get their shots. Now, it would include Richard, too. When they were all finally on their way to the county health department in the car, the older girls and Richard in the back seat, Lela, Charlie, Tommy and little Elizabeth in the front seat, the girls still sniffling and carrying on about there they were going. Charlie told them if they would take their shots and not cry, he would take them all to Mr. Stagg's hamburger joint and buy them each a hamburger.

Richard had never heard the word hamburger, so he did not

understand what was so grand that it would cause Faye to stop carrying on so, since she was known for her fear of everything.

The county health nurse was all the girls had told Richard she would be. She reminded him of a General lining up his troops for the front-line battle zone. He was so scared he scarcely felt the needle when he got his shot. He only knew that it was all over when baby Elizabeth stopped screaming so loud. They all piled back into the car and the next stop was a small gray building that looked like a boat to Richard. Charlie sat each child on a high stool and told the man to bring each of them a Grapette soda pop and a hamburger.

The smell alone was as near akin to heaven as Richard had ever imagined. He had never tasted anything like it. He was ashamed to ask for another one, but felt like he could eat a dozen without the slightest bit of trouble. Charlie noticed him looking longingly at the other children's unfinished food and told the cook, "My oldest boy could eat another one." Richard ate this one very slowly, savoring each delicious morsel.

Spring gave way to summer with a vengeance, and the work seemed like it was never done. When they were not busy in the fields, there was wood to cut for the fireplace and the cook stove. While Charlie was busy with the things that did not require help, Richard was always glad to do things for Lela. He gathered all the fruit and helped her peel it for canning. He enjoyed the smell of the cooking fruit, and he soon learned that what was left over from the day's canning would be made into one of Lela's good cobblers for supper.

Pearl was the scholar in the family. Her short bob of hair was so red it looked as if her head was on fire as she bent it continually over her books trying to study all the time that she was not busy helping with the younger children. She tried to teach Richard to read and was not put off in the least by his lack of interest in her efforts. As she followed him around while he was working, he would ruffle her hair and tell her, "If all the school teachers was as pretty as you, Pearl, I think I would go back to school."

After the work was finished every night, Richard and Tommy would sit in the dark on the back porch and play guessing games. Tommy's favorite was to guess how many points the big bright evening star had as they would sit and look at it high above the Persimmon tree in the back field.

Charlie told the children that the Fourth of July would be coming the next week and Mr. Steve Dowdy was planning a barbecue for all the neighborhood. If they were finished hoeing cotton, they would go.

On the morning of the fourth, all the children worked as hard as they could getting all the chores finished. Lela spent the morning baking a cake and some pies to carry to the barbecue. Shortly after noon the wash tub was carried onto the screened back porch and filled with water that had been warming in the hot sun all morning. Starting with Elizabeth, all the children were stood in the tub and scrubbed clean, then dressed in some of their better clothes, their hair brushed and their shoes shined.

The horses were hitched to the wagon loaded with all the food and ready to go. Charlie had also prepared the wagon with piles of quilts because he knew the little ones would most likely be drowsy before time to go home. It wasn't a long ride to Mr. Steve's pasture where the barbecue was being held, but the sleepyheads would be lulled into a deep sleep by the swaying wagon on those very quilts when the day was done.

The long tables under the big oak trees were already loaded with pies, cakes, and good home-baked bread. The ladies were busy making lemonade in large jugs to be served over the cracked ice Mr. Curtis Dowdy had gone to the ice plant to buy that very afternoon. Some of that ice would also be used to make ice cream.

Everyone was in a carefree mood. Richard joined a game of washers being played in the shade of a huge oak tree. The men gathered at the pit where Mr. Steve was roasting a whole calf. The spit slowly turned as the men talked of crops and politics. Mr. Roosevelt was running for president on his New Deal platform. Henry Pearson, the community half-wit, allowed as how they need a new deal since "no one liked the one they had now".

When supper was over and everyone had eaten their fill, it was growing dark. The young men hung lanterns in the trees as the Coker brothers, Ervin and Virgil, tuned up their instruments to play some square dance music. A round yellow full moon was rising as the young people chose partners for the dancing and games that were being played. The men sat on planks laid across blocks of wood, and the ladies sat on quilts spread on the ground so they could watch the small children amuse themselves with games.

Richard crowded between Charlie and Max Kidd. He did not care to join the games. It was enough for him to just be close to Charlie and listen to him talk with the other men.

On the way home, Richard and Ruth lay on a quilt in the bed of the wagon and watched the moon overhead as the horses plodded slowly down the dusty road. Richard was so content in his love for his new family, that he drifted off to sleep and Charlie had to wake him when they got to the barn so Richard could help unhitch the horses and carry the sleeping children into the house.

Lela decided since it was almost time for the summer protracted meeting that the children needed some new clothes. She had been saving her butter and egg money and had sold some hens to the peddler. She thought she had enough for Richard some new pants and a store-bought shirt. The small town of New Albany boasted only one good store which was owned by a Jewish couple, Mr. & Mrs. Sherman. Mr. Sherman was a pleasant little man with wavy black hair and dark, friendly eyes. When his wife was not around, Mr. Sherman was especially nice and helpful. Lela found just the right navy blue pants and a white shirt for Richard. As he started for the fitting room to try them on his path was blocked by Mrs. Sherman, "Boy, don't hold those clothes close to you, you dirty farmer!"

Richard turned to Mrs. Sherman with a hurt expression and was about to explain that he was not a dirty farmer when Mr.

Sherman snapped, "Sadie, get to the cash register right now before I lose my temper!"

But Mrs. Sherman couldn't leave well enough alone. When they had finished their shopping, Lela pulled out her meager amount of money and stood waiting while Mrs. Sherman rang up the sale with a smirk on her face. Peering over the counter at Lela's legs, Mrs. Sherman pretended to be helpful, "Mrs. Myrick, how about a new pair of hose for yourself?" Lela's face turned apple red and for the first time, Richard noticed the runs in Lela's old stockings. He realized she was spending her money on him instead of herself. Rage built in his chest toward the small ugly woman and he wanted to slap her tightly woven hair plumb off her smug head.

As Richard clenched his fists together, Lela drew her shoulders up and looked Mrs. Sherman straight in the eye and calmly said, "Well, no ma'am, I don't need any hose today, thank you." With her head held high, Lela took Richard's hand. And marched out the door leaving a bewildered Mr. Sherman wringing his hands.

The Protracted Meetings were soon underway led by the Reverend Brown who was a small man with a booming voice. Each night he always had a bench full of mourners seeking salvation. The old white church with its three rows of benches were filled so the men and boys sat on their wagon beds outside under the trees. They could hear Mrs. Flora Sneed's loud piano playing and Mr. Gip Parrish's voice rising above it in the familiar hymns. At invitations time, Mrs. Lula Hill and Mr. Gip always got happy and shouted.

About the middle of the week, Richard noticed a small white fuzzy dog following Mr. Elec and Mrs. Lula as they stopped their wagon under the trees near Charlie's wagon. Richard went over to help Mrs. Lula out of the wagon. As she stepped to the ground, the small dog grabbed her dress hem and sat back pulling with all his tiny might. Mr. Elec got a stick and ran the dog down the road toward home. "I told you to get rid of that dog, Lula. You can't do a thing with him. He tries to tear up everything." Lula did not bother to answer her husband, but kept walking toward the church fanning herself as hard as she could with her palm-leafed fan.

Rev. Brown's sermon that night was on the End of Time. As he told of the horrors of Hell, several women started to shout and Mrs. Lula went from one sinner to the next all over the church, begging them to turn loose of the Devil and be saved. As she passed the back door, a small fuzzy object hurtled through the doorway and caught hold of her dress hem. Lula came down the middle aisle of the church at a fast pace, dragging the dog who was pulling backward as hard as he could, growling deep in his throat. It was quite a sight.

About that time, Mrs. Lula's niece, Sybil Dowdy came down the aisle to be saved. Mrs. Lula, unaware of the dog on her tail, clapped her hands together and hollered, "Praise God, I've added another star to my crown!" People began to laugh and even

Rev. Brown couldn't help himself as he laughed until tears streamed down his cheeks. When Mrs. Lula realized what everyone was laughing about, she looked down at the determined dog and told him, "Well, I'll just swan to goodness!"

The rows of snowy white cotton seemed to stretch endlessly as the whole family bent their backs under the heavy picking sacks. Faye cried because she stuck a burr in her finger and made it bleed. She lay back on the sack sucking on her finger and watched a hawk drift high in the blue October sky

The nights had cooled so they had a small fire at night. After everyone had a bath, they all gathered before the fire for Charlie to read them a story from the Bible. He usually let them select which one they wanted to hear. Tommy always picked "Daniel in the Lion's Den". Pearl's favorite was the story of Ruth. When Charlie asked Richard if he had a favorite, he said, "Yessir. I would like to hear the story of Joseph." Charlie looked at the boy and wondered if he was thinking of his own family that he had chosen to leave in order to live.

Now that the last bale of cotton had been hauled to the gin, the weather was getting cold enough to butcher the hogs. Richard loved this time of year. his body was growing so fast he could eat half a dozen of Lela's biscuits with the good sausage she was making. She let Richard have the samples to tell her if they seasoning was right. After the meat had been packed in the long sacks Lela had made, they hung the sausage from the rafters of the smokehouse and built a smoldering fire in a drum. Richard volunteered to keep the fire just right to smoke the sausage. He coughed and choked as he stoked the fire with hickory shavings. His mouth watered at the good smell of the smoking meat. It seemed to him that he was hungry all the time.

After supper Charlie got the Sears Roebuck catalog and let the children see what Santa Clause was making at the North Pole. Each child had a favorite toy. Tommy wanted some toy soldiers. Ruth and Pearl wanted new clothes. Faye wanted a watch baby and Elizabeth was too young to even know what Christmas was all about.

Charlie saw Richard gazing at the pictures of the guns each night as he poured over the book, dreaming of a time when he would go hunting to kill some rabbits or squirrels for a good stew. One night after the other children had gone to bed and Richard was still turning the pages of the catalog, Charlie came into the room.

"Son, would you like Santa to bring you any certain thing?"

Richard raised clear blue eyes filled with tears, "No sir, I don't reckon I would. He has already brought me enough just being welcomed into this family." Charlie took the catalog and looked at the pages open to the guns. "Well, supposing that you wanted one of these, which one do you think would be best?" Richard pointed to the one that his heart had been set on and Charlie smiled, marking the page by turning down the corner of the page before closing the book.

Lela and the girls cleaned the house for top to bottom. Then they got out the red and green roping and hung it from each of the dining room's four corners. Where it met in the center, they hung a red paper bell.

Charlie, Richard, and Tommy hitched Prince to the sled and went to the woods to chop down a Christmas tree. They picked one that was tall and round with full boughs. Next, they stopped at the holly tree and Richard took his knife and cut large branches for Ruth and Pearl to make wreaths for the door and the windows.

The house smelled of starched linens and evergreen. Lela had started baking the Christmas cakes. When she finished one, she placed it inside the buffet on a shelf and closed the door so nothing could get to it. One of the cakes was decorated with coconut and candies. She did not count on Tommy's love for candy for when she went to place her famous Peach Cake in the buffet she found the coconut cake was missing some of its candy decorations. But she loved Tommy, so she couldn't spank him. Instead, she removed the remaining candy from the cake and gave it to him a few pieces at a time until it was all gone.

Bondy Bailey lived with his mother and father across the woods from Charlie and Lela. His wife had died in childbirth along with their first child. Being lonely for company of his own age, he would visit about twice a week. Darkness came early in December and one could see the light from Bondy's five-cell flashlight bobbing across the back fields as he walked along the path by the garden fence. The children always enjoyed his visits. Lela would get out the popcorn and fill the long-handled black popper that usually hung by the fireplace. She put a large gob of butter and the right about of corn in it and handed it to Richard. He got on his knees and held the popper over the open flame, shaking it all the time and soon the room was filled with the good smell of hot popcorn. Lela brought the dishpan and some more butter and salt. The popping continued until the dishpan was piled high with flaky white kernels.

The popcorn was placed on a small table and everyone gathered around it in a circle. Each one took handfuls and ate it while Bondy entertained the children with scary stories. Lots of times, Richard was afraid to go to bed after some of Bondy's realistic tales. Despite being scared, the stories were a highlight of Bondy's visits.

Because it was Christmastime, Bondy told Christmas stories on this particular visit. Tommy was amazed when Bondy said that on Christmas Eve all the animals could talk like humans and would get down on their knees at midnight and pray. Tommy wanted to go to the stable and see if the animals were indeed talking like humans, but Bondy told him it only happened on Christmas Eve, so he would have to wait until the next night.

Christmas Eve was spent killing the hen and cooking her in the pressure cooker, making bread for dressing, and getting the other dishes ready for the celebratory Christmas dinner. Lela always made vegetable soup and cornbread for supper on Christmas Eve, and she would open a jar of her canned peaches for dessert. She gave each child a small piece of plain cake to eat with the peaches. When the supper was over and the kitchen cleaned, they all played games until bedtime.

The small children, of course, were not in the least bit sleepy, but went reluctantly to bed early after placing a straight chair beside their beds so Santa would have a place to leave their Christmas presents.

When the children were finally asleep, Charlie came into the kitchen carrying a small wrapped package which he handed to Lela. When she opened it, tears sprang to her eyes for she had nothing to give Charlie. Although it was only two lace-trimmed handkerchiefs, Lela treasured them as though they cost a million dollars.

Charlie then snuck out to the barn and brought in the children's presents from their hiding spot. He placed each child's small amount of toys, fruit, and candy in their chair by their beds. When he finished, Lela came into the room to put the kettle of water by the fire. It was dark in the room except for the low flickering light from the flames dancing in the fireplace. Lela startled as she saw someone standing beside the Christmas tree.

Richard turned from the window and said, "I didn't mean to scare you, Miss Lela. I couldn't sleep so I came in here to look at the Christmas tree."

Lela pulled a rocker over close to the fire and sat down, She gestured for Richard to do the same. When he was seated, she told him, "It will soon be a year since you came to live with us. Do you wish you were with your own family?"

Richard raised concerned eyes to hers. "Oh, no ma'am. I

think of you as my family now and I can still see my brothers and sisters when I want to. No, Miss Lela, this has been the best year of my life! I do miss my mother, but you have been so much like a mother to me. I love you and Mr. Charlie like you were my mother and my father."

Lela rose and walked over to the rocker and put her arms around the young man, "And we love you, too, Richard. When a mother gives birth, she suffers the physical pain of having a child, but you came to be our child through your own pain and suffering. You are the son of our hearts."

Charlie came into the room carrying a long, wrapped parcel, intending to place it under the Christmas tree, but when he saw Richard and Lela at the hearth, he handed the package to Richard, saying, "Well, looks like Santa Claus can visit you now, Richard."

With trembling hands, Richard tore off the paper and could scarcely believe his own eyes. The shiny new Sear Roebuck rifle lay in his hands. Richard was so overcome with joy he flung himself into Charlie's arms. "Thank you! Thank you, Mr. Charlie!"

With tears of gladness filling his eyes, Charlie placed this arm around the boy that he had learned to love so well, "Merry Christmas, Son."

Shady Grove Civil War Nurse

The log church stood in the midst of a grove of large oak trees. Around the back, planks were nailed between the trees making a long table for spreading church dinners, as was the custom of those days.

To some, it was perhaps, a forbidding looking church, but to others it was a shady and serene place to worship on a Sunday morning. It was the shade created by these trees that gave the church its name, Shady Grove.

Even at that time, the cemetery at the church had graves dating back to the turn of the 19th century. Some said the unmarked mounds back in the wooded area behind the church were the graves of slaves that were brought by the early settlers from the

Carolinas, long before the War Between the States.

Not far from the side of the church lived a beautiful girl named Tennie. She was known and admired for her sweet ways and for helping tend to the sick and elderly when they were in need.

One Sunday during the war, the fighting was getting closer and closer to the community as Grant's army pushed into Northern Mississippi. The preacher at the church stood up and told the congregation, "People we had better pray. Word just came that the Yankees are just across Mud Creek."

Many among the congregation rushed from the church, hoping to get home in time to hide their food and livestock, since word had it that Grant's men were taking everything of use in their path.

While the remainder of the congregation prayed, a Yankee captain rode up to the church and interrupted the service, telling everyone that the Union Army was commandeering the church for use as a hospital. Before the congregation dispersed, the captain made a plea for nurses to help tend the wounded.

No one spoke until Tennie rose and said "I would be glad to volunteer, sir." Then a few more women from the group raised their hands to volunteer also.

Before long, the church was transformed into a makeshift hospital ward with blankets piled on the floor to act as beds for the wounded and dying. Tennie immediately took charge of the hospital and tended the wounds of the first soldier brought in.

As the battle at Mud Creek continued, more and more wounded were brought into the small church and Tennie worked tirelessly day and night to attend them all.

When the wounded died, Tennie traveled with the body to the cemetery, seeing the men put in their graves and saying prayers over them before they were buried. Though they were the enemy, Tennie said every boy was some mother's son and deserved a Christian burial.

As the weeks drug on, Tennie spent most of her days and nights at the church, breaking only at dusk to go home to bathe, snatch a few hours of sleep, and change clothes.

In the darkness, she would return to the church, picking her way through the woods by the light of a single candle she carried with her.

In the 1930s, long after the war was just a history-book memory, Tennie had lived a long and full life and passed away. Some boys were coming home from a party on a Saturday night. As they passed the cemetery, they happened to stop and there, moving among the headstones, was a shimmering form dressed in a long white Victorian dress, a single candle held high, as though the form searched for a friend or loved one among the long-forgotten graves.

For years, the boys told what they had seen. No one would walk past the cemetery late at night, especially not on a windy fall night when the moon was full, not when a scudding cloud could mask the moon, leaving just enough light to see the form of a young girl in a long white dress walking among the headstones, the flickering light from a single candle in her hand.

Cooper Family History

Reprint from the 1988-1993 Reunion Booklet

In the spring of 1988, Sue Cooper Rogers and Mable Myrick Gates got together and started kicking the idea around for a family reunion. We talked and wrote back and forth. Since Sue and Kenneth are farmers, we decided to have it in the fall.

We set the date and Sue contacted everybody. I have to give her credit for all the organization for the reunion. She did a wonderful job of organizing it, renting a building, and contacting everyone.

The first reunion was attended by 42 of Sanford and Elizabeth Cooper's grandchildren and great-grandchildren. It was such a success the next year that in 1989 we invited all the other cousins. These were Pa Cooper's brothers' children and grandchildren. We had a large number in attendance and everyone seemed to have a good time. Since then we have been meeting at the City Park building in Dresden on the fourth Saturday night in October of each year.

We try each year to do something a little different. This year I have written a story of how it might have happened that our grandparents were in Tennessee and how they could have gotten here.

I have always wanted to be a writer, so I have given our ancestors an interesting past. The beginning of this story is all fiction. We don't know for sure how they came to be in North Carolina, but let's just suppose that this is the way it could have happened.

My mother, Lela Cooper Myrick, always told me that her father Sanford Cooper told her that his great-grandfather came to North Carolina from Holland, that he was Dutchman whose name was William. So we will suppose that much is true. But to make for more interesting reading, I have given William a past that is pure fiction. His coming to America is a figment of my imagination, but we know he came here. So it could have happened just this way.

Before I start William's journey, let me say that all the dates starting with Ephrem and Louisa are correct. Sue Cooper Rogers and Ruby Tuck researched the past generation, starting with them.

The Cooper Family Story

January 14, 1823, a dapper little Dutchman named William Cooper stepped off a ship onto the docks of London. The morning was cold and foggy, and he was really hungry after his trip from Holland. He had come to England looking for work.

He entered the first establishment he came to looking for food and coffee. It was a common house with rooms to let upstairs and a large serving room. As he entered, a fire burned cheerily in a large stone fireplace, giving the room a warm and inviting look, despite the riffraff that loitered about.

William sat at a table near the fireplace and ordered coffee and a plate a food. He looked around the room full of sailors from ships docked on the Thames preparing to set sail for ports all over the world.

In the corner of the room, a sailor was plucking the strings of a lute and singing in a melancholy voice:

Black is the color of my true love's hair,
Her looks are something wonderous fair.
The purest eyes and softest hands,
I love the grass on where she stands.

William was so caught up in the sailor's song of "Greensleeves" he hardly noticed two men had sat down next to him, until the serving maid brought him his food.

The singing died away and William found himself listening as the two men talked of the voyage they would start in a few days.

The captain was a tall handsome young man who was a Colonial. William heard him tell the other man his home was in Charleston of the Carolinas, and he was getting ready to set sail for home. Without seeming too eager, William asked if there was work to be had in his homeland. The captain said if he was willing to work hard, there was good fortune to be made in building and farming. William inquired about how to book passage to this new land and the captain hired him as a deck hand.

The journey across the wild stretch of water was something William would never forget. He was so frightened at time, he feared never to see land again.

After weeks of being tossed about through storms and blinding rain, at dawn one morning, the lookout in the crow's nest high in the rigging shouted to the captain on the deck, "Land ho, Sir, off the starboard side!"

William took his place on deck with the other sailors. From what he had heard and read of this place, he was expecting to see a steaming coastal swamp; instead his first sight of land was a great forest.

As the ship docked, William held his breath at first sight of the white-washed city. It looked like a beautiful handful of pearls flung upon the sunlit beach. "So this is the Carolinas?" he asked the captain.

"Indeed, it is, lad."

To William it looked like paradise after the soot and fog of London.

William was one and twenty when he stepped off the ship into this lovely new country, and eager to make his fortune. After the purser paid all of them, William turned to one of the sailors and asked if he could tell him where he might find a room and maybe a job. He was directed to the home of a wheelwright who usually had work for people passing through Charleston.

Mr. Webb hired William after learning he had some experience repairing buggy wheels in his native Holland. He also told him of a boarding house near the waterfront where he might find a room cheap.

William strolled through the streets of Charleston. He could not believe how clean and white everything looked. He arrived at the address Mr. Webb had given him to find a dazzling white two-storied structure with wide porches all around. The upper porch formed a balcony with white painted ironwork. Flowers bloomed in gay profusion everywhere and a huge jasmine vine almost covered the upper porch.

Just as William was about to knock on the door, it was flung open by one of the prettiest girls he had ever seen. Her flowing red hair and green eyes seemed to shoot sparks as she stared at William and said, "Well, don't be standing there like you are daft, man. What might you be wanting?"

William finally found his tongue enough to say he was looking for a rom to rent. The girl led him through a large hallway with a winding staircase to the upper floor and back to a sitting room where a large raw-boned woman sat behind a desk totaling a column of figures in a ledger.

"This is Mrs. Bonds, the mistress of this house." The girl was turning to leave the room when the woman looked up and said, "Wait, Jenny, I have something for you to do. Now, what can I do for you, sir?" William asked about a room to let. When the arrangements were made, Jenny showed the room to William.

It was on the upper floor and sparsely furnished with a bed, chair, armoire, and small table by the bed with washbasin, pitcher, and candle stand. William walked to the window where he could look far out to sea. The salt breeze smelled clean, and William was glad he had come to this new land.

Time passed quickly as William worked long hours every day in Mr. Webb's shop repairing and making wheels at the large iron forge. If he had any spare time, he worked as a helper on a new building that was to be a warehouse near the Charleston harbor. Each night at supper he waited for the sight of Jenny as she helped serve the evening meal.

One night after supper, William sat on the porch taking his evening pipe and looking far out to sea. He was sometimes lonely for the family he had left in Holland, but this new world was full of excitement.

Jenny stepped out on the porch and William stood and asked if he might take her walking on the beach. They strolled along the water's edge and talked as a bright full moon made a silver path across the waves.

Jenny had come to Charleston from Ireland to live with her aunt only to find her gone, she knew not where. So, she had gotten work at Mrs. Bonds' boarding house as a maid.

As the weeks went by, Jenny and William fell in love. One day, Mr. Webb asked William if he would go to Asheville, North Carolina and deliver some wagon parts to a merchant there. William had heard that you could get a homestead there by staking claim and living on it for a year. He made the arrangements with Mr. Webb. When he went home that night, he told Jenny that he was going to North Carolina and asked if she would marry him and go along.

In a few days they were married in the small church that Jenny had attended since coming to Charleston. The few friends they had come to bring gifts for their journey and to wish them well.

The trip through the mountains was long and scary. Others going to seek their fortunes and build a homestead joined them. They lived in one of the wagons called a Conestoga, built like a room to hold all their bedding and cooking utensils. The front wheels were smaller than the back ones and painted a bright red. Other wagons were taken apart and piled atop one wagon with spare parts strapped in place by rope to deliver to the merchant in

Asheville. This was pulled by the wagon they rode in with a span of mules.

North Carolina was beautiful country. Soon William and Jenny found just the spot for their homestead. They lived in the wagon until they could get a crude cabin built out of logs. They planted a late garden. The season was good and they grew corn and potatoes for winter. Jenny went into the forest and found wild grape vines loaded with fruit, wild berries that she gathered for making pies and jelly.

The little storeroom was bursting with supplies they had raised and gathered when the cold winds of winter came.

William found work at building and in his spare time he built onto cabin so Jenny could have a kitchen and a sitting room. Time flew by with work and social gatherings at the little church that Jenny insisted they attend.

The preacher was a young man that had befriended William and Jenny.

In the winter of 1824, Jenny told William they were going to have a child. Jenny sewed and worked around the cabin waiting for her baby to be born. At night William carved and whittled. At first Jenny couldn't guess what he was making, but it soon became a beautiful cradle for the baby.

In the spring of 1825 Jenny gave birth to a healthy baby boy. As William stood looking down at his wife and son, he asked, "What shall we call him?" Jenny replied, "His name shall be Ephrem, the same as Joseph's son in the Bible because it means

'God has made me fruitful in a strange land."

Ephrem grew into a young man; it seemed to Jenny all too soon. By this time the homestead had prospered and William had built a nice home out of native mountain rock, taking the first crude cabin for a harness room for their horses.

Ephrem had a talent for raising and breaking horses. He had a nice buggy and a pair of matched Morgans. Their beautiful brown coats looked like satin and with their black manes and tails flowing in the wind, he was a sight to behold as he drove recklessly around the countryside.

The new parson had a lovely daughter named Louisa. Reverend Davis didn't care much for Ephrem, but he could see Louisa was as taken with him just as he had been with her mother. After months of courting, Ephrem asked Louisa if she would marry him and go on an adventure. He told her he was thinking of joining the wagon train going to Tennessee. He had heard that the soil was so rich you could grow anything. He had also heard a good crop for that area was said to be tobacco.

With much tears and sorrow, William and Jenny watched as a wagon was made ready for the journey. They gave them gifts of cooking utensils and bedding and packed the wagon with light pieces of furniture for their new home in Tennessee.

Louisa was used to hard times, being a preacher's daughter. She had to adapt to most any lifestyle at hand.

The journey started pleasantly enough, but as the wagons climbed higher into the chain of mountains, Louisa became apprehensive. As she sat on the high spring seat, she pulled her bonnet down over her eyes. The narrow pass through the mountain was hardly wide enough for them to pass through. One misstep would plunge them end over end into oblivion.

Louisa could not see the bottom of the mountain gorge, so she closed her eyes and prayed. After what seemed like days, she heard water running swiftly and she opened her eyes to see they had come out of the mountain pass and were crossing a swiftly running stream.

For many days they drove on. At night they camped near the streams. Finally, one day they came to a sign that said Gibson County. They stopped near a place called Rutherford, Tennessee. They found a grove of trees outside the town and made camp. Ephrem went to inquire about work and to get some supplies.

Louisa set the spider for cooking over the fire and baked bread and fried meat. Supper was ready when Ephrem returned with good news. He told Louisa he thought they would stay. He had inquired and found out that they could work as laborers in the fields helping to harvest tobacco and other crops.

Ephrem and Louisa worked hard and the next year they applied for a homestead. In the spring of 1850 they moved into a cabin on their land. As soon as the few pieces of furniture they had brought from North Carolina were in place and supplies were on the table, Louisa told Ephrem she had something to tell him. She was expecting a child.

Louisa worked hard all spring and summer, making the

cabin into a home and sewing for the coming child. So on August 14, 1850 her son was born. They named him William Benjamin Cooper after his grandfather. As time passed, they were blessed with another son they named John.

Ephrem worked hard and soon he was raising tobacco and other crops. As always, he loved to breed and raise Morgan horses. The little boys loved to help take care of the horses. Ephrem supplemented their income by training and selling these beautiful horses.

When William was eleven, war came to the South. Grant's soldiers made a sweep through Tennessee, taking everything in their path. Ephrem had just broke to ride one of the most beautiful Morgans he had ever raised. He could hardly stand to see it confiscated for the Northern cause.

The years of the war were full of hardship and suffering. Ephrem fought in several skirmishes around the homestead. There as talk of raising a unit, but nothing came of it. After the Northern soldiers came through and took everything, the people were so scattered just trying to help each other survive.

The war finally ended, but reconstruction was cruel to everyone. Taxes were so high it was all Ephrem and Louisa could do to hold on to their home.

Ephrem had a talent for making harnesses and repairing wheels, so he opened a blacksmith shop to help his income. Since no one could afford to pay for field work, each man helped his neighbors and in return his neighbors helped him back.

Little by little things got better and in the spring of 1870 William, being a young man of twenty, went courting a neighbor girl named Sarah Pickens. Louisa knew he had asked if he could bring her home for Sunday dinner that William was in love. So, on August 28, 1870, they were married in Gibson County, Tennessee.

This union was soon blessed by a son they named after his grandfather, Ephrem Sanford Cooper, born June 28, 1871. As the years passed, they were blessed by six more children: Newt, John, James, Gentry, Alice, and Molly. The passing years were filled with work and much love, along with life's tears and sorrows.

Sanford was one to look around, so while he was visiting a friend he met the beautiful Nancy Elizabeth Myrick. He soon fell in love with Lizzie, as he fondly nicknamed her, and they were married on February 25, 1892.

They settled a few miles outside the small town of Dresden, Tennessee, where they raised their family.

Sanford was an industrious man. Working at several trades, he accumulated some wealth for a man of his day. He built Lizzie a large, two-storied white house that sat on a small rise. It had wide porches all around and was an ideal place for children to play beneath the shades of towering cedars and oaks.

Sanford stayed busy all the time and saw to it that the children did, too. He built a barn that had an added room over a spring and used this to slaughter cattle and hogs for the public. It was said that his hands were never idle. At night he mended harnesses and made whips that he plaited out of the hides of the cattle. He soaked them in a secret formula that made them into leather.

Sanford and Elizabeth were blessed with eleven children: Jasper, Rosie, Frank, Lula, Fred and Ed, Albert, Lela, Walter, Beulah, and Ruby.

Lizzie was known far and wide for the good cook that she was. They brought their children up to work and attend church. Sanford was one to see his family in church every meeting day at McClain's Chapel.

The children were growing up, getting married, and leaving home. William and Sarah came to visit in the spring of 1917. He had been sick all winter and couldn't seem to feel much better. He took worse while they were there and he died on April 15, 1917.

That same year, World War I started, and many young men from Dresden and surrounding communities had to go. Among them were Sanford and Lizzie's son Frank. He was just in training that fall in New Jersey, when he took measles and pneumonia and died October 6, 1918. Two soldiers came back to Dresden with his body for burial. Everyone was grief-stricken. Frank was so young and full of life. He was the funny one. It was said he could even play any tune on an instrument. Lela said that he could even play a tune on a hand saw.

Almost every night, before the war, Frank went to the black share-cropper house to play music with their boys. It was said that they came to the back door with caps in hand, inquiring if they could come in and see "Mr. Frank". Lizzie brought them to the parlor where Frank's casket was and told them to look at him. One of the boys named Jim burst into tears and said, "Law me, Miz Lizzie, we can't stand it. Mr. Frank was the life of us. We won't never have no more fun with him gone. You know how we loved him."

They asked if they could come to the funeral and Sanford told them they could. They stood outside the small white Methodist church called McClain's Chapel as Frank's body was lowered into the red clay earth beside his grandfather William.

The years passed but Lizzie never got over his death. She kept his clothes hanging in the downstairs closet until they rotted and fell onto the floor.

In 1921, Sarah died and was laid to rest next to William and Frank at McClain's Chapel Cemetery. During this time, another beloved son of Sanford and Lizzie died. Ed was killed in a car wreck.

The years passed with their joys and sorrows. On June 28, 1936, Sanford had a birthday dinner. All the children and grandchildren came to help him celebrate. A man from town came out in the afternoon to make a family picture. There were 45 family members gathered for the occasion. Not long after that, Sanford fell into failing health and because of no known treatment for diabetes at that time, his mind became confused.

Lizzie had a hard time trying to keep up with him on countless occasions and had to call her son Walter to go and get his father from wherever he had wandered off to. After a long illness, he died on November 20, 1941. It soon became apparent that Lizzie couldn't stay alone in the country, so she sold her house and bought one in Dresden close to her son Walter.

She never had to stay one night alone, thanks to the love of her granddaughter Sue Cooper Rogers, who gave up her time of being a child to stay with her grandmother every night all through Sue's growing up and teenage years. She gave Lizzie a gift that not one of the rest of us was willing to give, her time and love. Lizzie died March 20, 1952.

I am proud to be named for you grandmother and thank you for being the Godly Christian woman that you were. I know each of us can quote Proverbs 31:10, 31 that describes you so well. *Proverbs 31: 10—Who can find a virtuous woman her price is far above rubies. Proverbs 31:31—Give her of the fruits of her hands and let her own works praise her in the gates.*

I love you, Grandmother,
Mable Elizabeth Myrick Gates

Lela's Family Recipes

RECIPE INDEX ON PAGE 123

The following pages contain many of the recipes which were cooked time and again by the women in this family. The house always smelled of something on the stove or in the oven. If perhaps, a visitor happened by between mealtimes, the air most likely still held a hint of the last meal cooked and leftovers would readily be doled out for any hungry belly.

The cakes, pies, and pastries were a delightful addition to days of celebration and a special part of those "regular days" in between. A pan of biscuits was most likely the first thing the daughters learned to cook because Lela's biscuits were not only a staple in the home, but were famous among the community (for proof re-read The Country Doctor).

We hope you will try these recipes and that doing so will bring joy to you and your friends and family for years to come.

Savory Dishes/Kitchen Essentials

Lela's Biscuits

Sift large bowl full of **self-rising flour**. Make a well in center and put into this well:

1 ¼ cups **buttermilk**
2 heaping tablespoons **lard**

Mix with hands into a stiff dough. Roll out on floured surface, cut with biscuit cutter. Melt 1-2 tablespoons of lard in pan you are going to cook them in, tilt pan so lard will pool in one corner. Dip tops of biscuits in melted lard as you place them in pan. Cook at 400° until slightly browned.

How to Make Lard—Lela Cooper Myrick

When hog is cut up, remove fat from all pieces, cut into small pieces in a wash pot or some other pot. Start small fire under pot stirring with wooden paddle constantly. Keep fire low under pot. Cook until all pieces float to top. Pull fire away from pot. Pin clean cloth over lard can with clothespins. Dip lard out of pot and strain into clean lard can, drop pieces of cooked meat from cloth into small bucket to make crackling bread from. Put lid on can and store in cool place until ready to use.

Green Tomato Relish —Lela Cooper Myrick

1 gallon green tomatoes (chopped)
1 quart onions (chopped)
1 quart cucumber (chopped)
9 pounds hot pepper (chopped)
½ cup salt
1 quart vinegar
3 cups sugar
1 box turmeric
1 box mustard
4 cups flour

Mix all ingredients together in a large pot that will not stick.
Cook on medium heat until all ingredients are tender and can be mashed. Scald jars and lids and let dry (or dry in warm oven).
Can and seal jars.

Ripe Tomato Relish —Lela Cooper Myrick

6 pounds ripe tomatoes
2 hot peppers, chopped finely
2 cups sugar
2 teaspoons all spice
9 medium onions, chopped finely
3 cups vinegar
salt to taste

Cook till it thickens. Can and seal in sterile jars.

Dill Pickles—Sudie Cooper

Scrub cucumber (medium size) and place in quart jars. Add dill head and lump alum. Bring to a rolling boil ½ cup pickling salt and one quart white vinegar and two quarts water. Pour over cucumbers and seal. Put in a water bath cooker. Let water come to a boil. Turn off hear and let jars stay in cooker ten minutes. When removing from water bath place on towel and cover with a towel until they cool.

Old Way to Can Green Beans—Lela Cooper Myrick

1 gallon broken green beans
½ cup vinegar
½ cup sugar
¼ cup canning salt

In open pan, cook at rolling boil for one hour. Pack in hot sterile jars, then seal.

Canned Sausage—Lela Cooper Myrick

When sausage is ground, make out into patties. Cook until done. Have jars clean, dry, and hot. Pack sausage in jars, pour grease over sausage that you cooked out of sausage. Put lids on and seal.

Canned Beef—Lela Cooper Myrick

Cut beef into pieces. Put steaks together so they can be cooked together. Roast will have to be cut into pieces. Scrap beef cut from close to the bone will be used for soups.

Heat small amount of lard in skillet, put meat in skillet just long enough to sear on both sides. Into hot, sterile jars, pack meat. Add about ½ cup of water. Put lids on and put in pressure cooker. Prepare 40 minutes at 15 pound pressure. Continue until all meat is canned. Meat can then be opened and rolled in flour and browned, use juice in jar to make gravy.

Spiced Peaches—Lela Cooper Myrick

1 dish pan peaches, peeled
1 cup vinegar
6 cups sugar
2 tablespoons mixed pickling spices

Pour enough water to cover peaches in to pot. Cook peaches on high heat until tender. Pour in hot, sterile jars, cover with liquid and seal.

Colored Butter Beans —Lela Cooper Myrick

Shell and wash beans. Cook on medium heat for at least two hours. Cook piece of steak of loin or ham, with beans. The longer you cook them is better. When they are done mix a tablespoon flour with ¼ cup water, beat until smooth. Pour into butter beans, stirring constantly. Cook for a few minutes longer.

Goulash —Lela Cooper Myrick

Cook 8 ounces elbow macaroni until tender and drain. Brown one pound ground beef, then drain. Add one large can tomato sauce. Place in a casserole dish, stir to mix, then place American cheese slices on top of dish and bake at 350° until cheese is melted.

Chicken + Dumplings —Lela Cooper Myrick

Cut chicken into serving pieces, place in large pan, cover with water, salt to taste. Put foil tightly over pan, bake at 400° for 1 ½ hours.

For dumplings, sift 2 cups self-rising flour into medium sized bowl. Make well in flour. In small bowl sift ¾ cups flour, 1 cup of hot water, beat with a fork until smooth. Pour into well of flour in large bowl. Mix by hand until dough is stiff. Pinch off small amounts and roll really thin on a floured surface. Cut strips and place on plate near stove until all dumplings are rolled out and cut.

Drain chicken broth off cooked chicken into large pot. When chicken broth comes to a rolling boil, start dropping dumplings in and stir down with large spoon, gently, until all are dropped in. Remove from heat, put tight lid on pot until served. Serve as soon as possible after cooking.

Bar-B-Q Chicken "That's Different"
—Lela Cooper Myrick

½ cup of tomato catsup
½ cup of French dressing
large onion

Cut up chicken in serving pieces. Roll in flour and place in baking dish. Salt and pepper to taste. Mix catsup and French dressing, pour over chicken. Slice onion and place on chicken. Cover with foil tightly. Bake at 350° for 1 ½ hours. Serve with country fried potatoes.

Pearl's Sweet Potato Casserole – Pearl Myrick Hill

3 cups sweet potatoes, cooked
1 stick butter
½ cup sugar
2 eggs, beaten
1/3 cup milk
1 tsp Vanilla

Mix all ingredients well, and place in casserole dish

Topping:
1 cup light brown sugar
1 cup chopped pecans
½ cup melted butter
½ cup flour

Cream together & sprinkle on top of casserole.
Bake at 350 for 25 minutes

Chicken Casserole – Louisa Cooper Colleur

Boil **fryer-size chicken** until tender, remove all meat from the bones. Mix can of **celery soup**, can of **cream of chicken soup**, 2 cups **chicken broth** (you can use more if you need to to make your dressing thinner), ¼ cup **milk**, small chopped **onion**, 3 cups **corn bread crumbs**, 2 slices of **toasted bread** or **biscuits** crumbled (2 or 3), 1 teaspoon **sage**, ½ teaspoon **salt** and ½ teaspoon **black pepper**. Mix real good. Grease baking dish with oleo. Put layer of dressing in bottom of dish. Lay chicken pieces over dressing. Pour rest of dressing over chicken. Cover with foil and back 40 minutes on 400°. Take off foil and dot with oleo. Cook 15 minutes without foil.

Chop Suey — Thomas Myrick

1 ½ lbs Ground Chuck
1 Can Chop Suey Vegetables
1 Can Bean Sprouts
2 TSP Corn Starch
Olive Oil

1 Small Onion, Diced
3 Stalks Celery, Chopped
1 Can Water Chestnuts
Chinese Noodles
Cooked Rice

Soften the onion and celery in olive oil in Dutch oven, add Ground Chuck and brown, drain, add all veggies (drain cans first). Cook 20 minutes, add corn starch, cook 10 minutes more. Serve over rice, top with crispy Chinese noodles.

This recipe was re-created and submitted by Brenda Dowdy Bell, from memory (helped by recipes found on the internet). "I can remember going to Uncle Thomas & Aunt Melvie's and he would cook this. I was inspired to re-create this fond memory.")

Desserts/Sweet Stuff

Lela's Basic Cake

She used this recipe for all her cakes and frosted them with different frostings (recipes to follow).

2 cups self-rising flour
1 ½ cups sugar
2 eggs
½ cup shortening, melted
1 ¼ milk
1 teaspoon vanilla

Fresh Coconut Frosting—Lela Cooper Myrick

Drain milk from fresh coconut. (Poke coconut "eyes" with ice pick.) Add 1 ½ cups sugar and cook until syrup forms a ball when dropped in cold water. Remove coconut shell and skin; grate or bring the white meat. Beat 2 egg whites until stiff. Beat into coconut syrup. Spread on cooled Basic Cake. Sprinkle coconut between layers and on top and sides of cake.

Caramel Frosting – Lela Cooper Myrick

2 cups sugar
1 can evaporated milk (not condensed milk)
1 tsp vanilla

Cook on medium heat until it forms a ball when dropped in cold water. Frost cake. this recipe can be used for chocolate cake by added ¼ cup cocoa.

Pappy Myrick's Favorite White Icing
—Lela Cooper Myrick

Cook 1 ½ cups sugar and 1 cup water into a stiff syrup. Beat at least 2 egg whites and add to syrup. Punch holes in cake and then frost.

Dried Peach Frosting – Lela Cooper Myrick
(Frosting for Basic Cake)

Simmer dried peaches in water until skins will come off. Peel and cook until they can be mashed. Add 1 ½ cups sugar and simmer until spreading consistency. Stir often to prevent scorching. When cool, use to ice Basic Cake.

Strawberry Cake – Linda Myrick Smith
(Using 3 Layers of Lela's Basic Cake)

Sweeten 1-2 cups of mashed fresh strawberries. Spread evenly over cooled cake layers. Ice cake with strawberry icing or Pappy's Favorite White Icing.

Chocolate Cake—Lela Cooper Myrick

Sift together 1 ½ cups self-rising flour, 1 teaspoon baking soda, 1 teaspoon salt, 1 cup sugar, ⅓ cup cocoa. Add ½ cup shortening, ½ cup buttermilk, 1 teaspoon vanilla, 1 egg. Beat together, add ½ up hot water, and mix thoroughly. Bake at 350° in a 9x11 pan for 30-45 minutes.

Icing: Cook 1 cup milk, 2/4 cup sugar, a heaping tablespoon cocoa to the soft ball stage. Beat in ½ stick margarine or butter. Poke holes in cake to allow icing to moisten it.

Orange Cake—Lela Cooper Myrick

2 cups self-rising flour
1 ½ cups sugar
½ cup shortening
2 eggs
1 teaspoon vanilla
1 ½ cups milk

Separate eggs. Set whites aside for icing. Mix all remaining ingredients and beat until smooth. Grease and flour 3 round cake pans. Pour equal amounts of batter in each pan. Bake at 350°.

For icing squeeze juice and pulp from 4 oranges. Add 2 cups of sugar. Cook until mixture is as stiff as molasses. Beat egg whites until stiff. When orange molasses is cooled, beat into egg whites. Punch holes in each layer before you frost.

Pound Cake — Effie Gates

4 eggs
1 ½ sugar
1 stick margarine or butter, melted
2 cups flour
1 tablespoon vanilla

Mix together. Batter will be very stiff. Cook on 350° in a bunt pan until done — about 35 minutes or until a toothpick comes out clean.

Fruit Cocktail Cake — Faye Myrick Dowdy
(Brenda Dowdy Bell doesn't remember where this recipe came from originally, but remembers it being good and so easy and they ate a million of them.)

2 cups self-rising flour
1 ½ cups sugar
2 eggs
1 can fruit cocktail with juice
1 teaspoon vanilla

Mix and bake in a 13x9 pan for 30 minutes at 350°.

Icing: 1 stick margarine, ¾ cup sugar, ½ cup milk, ½ vanilla. Cook 3 minutes, put on cake, and top with coconut, if desired.

Fruit Cocktail Cake—Eva Cooper

Cake:
1 ½ cups sugar
2 cups cake flour
2 teaspoons soda
½ teaspoons salt
2 eggs
303 can fruit cocktail

Pre-baked Topping:
½ cup chopped pecans
½ cup brown sugar

Final Topping:
1 stick oleo
½ cup Pet milk
¾ cup sugar
1 cup coconut

Mix all together and pour in greased Pyrex pan. On top put the ½ cup pecans and ½ cup brown sugar mixed together. Cook at 325° for 40 minutes. After, melt the oleo Pet milk and sugar in a pan and let boil 2 minutes. Remove from heat and add 1 cup coconut. Spread on cake and refrigerate.

Pound Cake—Susie Cooper

2 cups sugar
4-5 eggs
1 cup Wesson oil
1 teaspoon vanilla
1 cup milk
2 cups self-rising flour

Mx together first four ingredients. Add alternately milk and flour. Bake in greased Bundt pan 40-45 minutes or until firm at 350°.

Carrot Cake — Oneta Cooper

3 cups grated carrots
4 eggs, unbeaten
2 cups sugar
1 ½ cups Wesson oil

2 teaspoons soda
½ teaspoon salt
2 cups self-rising flour

Mix with electric mixer the carrots, eggs, sugar, and oil. Beat together ingredients until mixed. Add remaining ingredients, beat well. Pour into well-oiled and floured 9-inch pans. Bake at 350° for 40-45 minutes. Cool.

Icing:
8 ounces cream cheese
1 box powdered sugar

Soften the cream cheese to room temperature. Bet until fluffy and gradually beat in powdered sugar. Add a small amount of milk, if needed

Ding Dong Cake — Sue Cooper Rogers

Bake Duncan Hines Devil's Food Cake in 2 layers as directed on box. Cool, remove from pans, and slice into 4 layers with a knife.

Mix 1 package softened cream cheese, 1 container cool whip, and 1 box powdered sugar. Put between layers, but not on top.

Use 1 can Duncan Hines Chocolate Cake Frosting to ice cake. Refrigerate.

Carrot Cake—Hazel Myrick Davis

4 eggs
2 cups sugar
2 cups self-rising flour
3 cups grated carrots
1 ½ cups oil

2 teaspoons cinnamon
¼ teaspoon salt
½ cup flour
1 cup broken pecans

In a large bowl, beat the eggs, sugar, and oil at medium speed for about 2 minutes. Sift flour, salt, and cinnamon. Roll pecans in the flour and add to mixture. Stir in carrots and mix well. Bake in a 9x13 greased and floured pan at 350° for about 35 minutes.

Frosting:
1 8-ounce package cream cheese
1 stick butter or margarine, softened
1 ½ boxes confectioner's sugar
1 teaspoon vanilla

Mix and spread on cake when cooled.

Cream of Coconut Cake—Hazel Myrick Davis

1 box yellow cake mix
1 can cream of coconut
1 8-ounce carton sour cream

¼ cup oil
3 eggs

Mix all ingredients with mixer until smooth. Bake in greased and floured Bundt pan on 350° for 50 minutes.

Chess Pie—Faye Myrick Dowdy

1 ½ cups sugar
½ cup milk
3 eggs
1 stick margarine

1 tablespoon flour
1 tablespoon cornmeal
1 tablespoon vanilla
2 small pie shells

Soften margarine and mix together all ingredients. Bake at 300° about 30 minutes.

Fried Chocolate Pies—Lela Cooper Myrick

Use biscuit dough for crust. Chill dough before using. In a medium bowl mix ½ cups brown sugar and 1 heaping tablespoon of cocoa, "mix well". Pinch off small amount of dough and roll into a small circle on floured wax paper. Put tablespoon of chocolate mix in center of dough. Add a few dots of butter. Fold over and seal edges with fork. Fry on med-high heat until brown, flip over, fry on other side until brown.

Chocolate Pies—Sue Cooper Rogers
(Makes 2)

2 ½ cups sugar
3 heaping tablespoons flour
2 ½ tablespoons cocoa

5 egg yolks
1 ¼ cups water + 1/3 cup
2 tablespoons oleo

Mix and cook on top of stove until thick. Pour in a baked pie crust and cover with meringue.

Pecan Pie — Linda Myrick Smith

1 cup sugar
1 cup white Karo (light)
1/3 cup butter
¼ tsp salt
1 deep dish crust (unbaked)

1½ cups pecans (halved or chopped)
1 teaspoon vanilla
4 eggs, beaten

Combine sugar, Karo syrup, and butter in medium sauce pan and cook over low heat. Stir constantly until sugar dissolves and butter melts. Let cool slightly. Add eggs, vanilla, and salt. Stir well. Pour filling into pastry shell. Top with pecans. Bake at 325° 50-60 minutes (Alternate: Dump pecans into shell and pour filling over them.)

Egg Custard Pie — Lela Cooper Myrick

2 eggs
1 ½ cups milk
1 teaspoon vanilla

2 tablespoons flour
1 cup sugar + ½ cup
1 stick butter

Separate eggs, setting aside whites for meringue. In double boiler, mix and cook other ingredients until it thickens. Stir in ½ stick butter. Pour in unbaked pie crust and cook on 350° until crust is done. Beat whites with ½ cup sugar, added gradually. Spread on pie and brown in oven.

Chocolate Custard Pie—Lela Cooper Myrick

Follow directions for Egg Custard and add 2 tablespoons cocoa.

Peach Pie Filling—Lela Cooper Myrick

2 gallons peaches, unpeeled
½ cup vinegar
6 cups sugar

Mix sugar and vinegar with peaches. Let syrup rise. Mash and cook on low heat until done. Cool and freeze in boxes to make pies.

Chocolate Delight
—Ramona McLeod, daughter of Louisa Cooper Colleur

Bottom Layer: Mix together and line bottom of baking dish, bake at 350° for 15 minutes: 1 cup self-rising flour, 1 stick oleo (melted), and 1 cup chopped nuts.

Second Layer: Mix together and place on cooled crust: 1 cup confectioner's sugar, 8-ounce cream cheese (room temperature), and ½ cup Cool Whip.

Third Layer: Prepare two 4-ounce packages of instant chocolate pudding using directions on box. Spread on top of cream cheese layer.

Top with remaining Cool Whip and sprinkle with chopped nuts. Chill well before serving.

Apple Bread —Hazel Myrick Davis

2 cups self-rising flour
½ cup oil
½ cup milk
1 teaspoon cloves
2/3 cup pecans

1 cup sugar
1 egg
1 teaspoon cinnamon
2 cups chopped apples

Mix all and bake in a loaf pan on 350° for about an hour.

Lela's Teacakes

Make a well in 2 cups sifted self-rising flour; add the following:

¾ cup melted margarine
1 cup sugar
1 egg
½ teaspoon vanilla

Mix until dough is stiff and smooth. Roll out real thin on floured wax paper. Cut out with biscuit cutter, place on greased sheet pan, and bake at 350° until barely brown. Cool on wax paper.

Fruitcake Cookies—Mable Elizabeth Myrick Gates

Cream together ½ cup butter, 1 ¾ cups flour, and 3 eggs. Mix 3 cups flour, ½ teaspoon salt, 1 tablespoon cinnamon, and 1 teaspoon nutmeg. Gradually add dry ingredients to the egg mixture. Dissolve ½ teaspoon baking soda in ¼ cup warm water and add to the mixture. Chop 3 boxes of whole pitted dates. Add dates, 1 pound mixed candied fruit, 3 cups chopped pecans, and 1 tablespoon vanilla. This recipe makes 7 or 8 dozen cookies. It's easier to mix with your hands because the dough is stiff. (Pre-chopped dates won't give the moist, chewy cookie that you get by chopping them yourself. If the dates stick together, dust them with a little flour.) Drop by teaspoons on greased cookie sheets. Bake on 350° until lightly golden.

Haystacks—Hazel Myrick Davis

½ cup Pet milk
2 cups sugar
20 marshmallows
1 cup chopped nuts
1 stick butter or oleo
1 ½ cups graham crackers
1 cup coconut

Cook butter, sugar, and milk for three minutes. Remove from heat, add marshmallows. Stir until melted, add coconut, nuts, and graham cracker crumbs. Mix and drop spoonfuls onto wax paper. Allow to cool/set before serving.

Potato Chip Cookies —Hazel Myrick Davis

1 cup melted butter
1 cup sugar
2 ½ cups sifted flour
2 cups rushed potato chips
1 cup packed brown sugar

2 eggs, well beaten
1 cup chopped nuts

Preheat oven to 350°. Combine butter, sugar, and eggs in a large mixing bowl until smooth. Add remaining ingredients, mix well. Drop by teaspoonfuls onto greased cookie sheet. Bake 12-15 minutes. Cookies will appear not done when first remove from the oven.

Chocolate Cobbler —Linda Myrick Smith

Heat oven to 350°. Melt ½ stick butter in an 8x8 pan. BATTER: ¾ cup sugar, 1 cup self-rising flour, ½ cup milk, 2 TBSP cocoa, 1 TSP vanilla. Mix together and pour in melted butter from the pan. Combine it all and return to the 8x8 pan. TOPPING: 1 cup sugar, 2 TBSP cocoa. Sprinkle over batter. Pour 1 cup hot water over top. Bake for 30 minutes. (Double for a 13x9 pan.)

Peach Cobbler —Pearl Myrick Hill

29 ounce can of peaches in light syrup, drained
1 cup milk
1 cup self-rising flour
1 cup sugar
1 stick butter
Teaspoon or two of cinnamon

Preheat oven to 350°. Drain peaches & set aside. Melt butter in 8x8 pan, (just stick it in the oven when preheating). Mix together flour, sugar, and cinnamon until blended. Pour in milk and stir until blended again. After butter is melted, take out of the oven and pour batter on top of butter, but don't stir! Use a big spoon and kind of set your peaches down all over the top of the batter, DON'T STIR. They will sink down and it will all be fine. Just distribute them as best you can but don't move them around once you set them down. If you want, sprinkle about a tablespoon of sugar and another teaspoon of cinnamon over the top of everything

Bake for 45-55 minutes or until its set in the center and golden.

RECIPE INDEX

SAVORY

LELA'S BISCUITS	100
HOW TO MAKE LARD	100
GREEN TOMATO RELISH	101
RED TOMATO RELISH	101
DILL PICKLES	101
HOW TO CAN GREEN BEANS	102
CANNED SAUSAGE	102
CANNED BEEF	103
SPICED PEACHES	103
COLORED BUTTER BEANS	104
GOULASH	104
CHICKEN + DUMPLINGS	105
BBQ CHICKEN "THAT'S DIFFERENT"	105
SWEET POTATO CASSEROLE	106
CHOP SUEY	107

SWEET

LELA'S BASIC CAKE	109
FRESH COCONUT FROSTING	109
CARAMEL FROSTING	110
PAPPY'S FAVORITE WHITE ICING	110
DRIED PEACH FROSTING	110
STRAWBERRY CAKE	110
LELA'S CHOCOLATE CAKE	111

RECIPE INDEX

SWEET CONTINUED

LELA'S ORANGE CAKE	111
EFFIE'S POUND CAKE	112
FAYE'S FRUIT COCKTAIL CAKE	112
EVA'S FRUIT COCKTAIL CAKE	113
SUSIE'S POUND CAKE	113
ONETA'S CARROT CAKE	114
DING DONG CAKE	114
HAZEL'S CARROT CAKE	115
CREAM OF COCONUT CAKE	115
CHESS PIE	116
FRIED CHOCOLATE PIES	116
CHOCOLATE PIES (2)	116
PECAN PIE	117
EGG CUSTARD PIE	117
CHOCOLATE EGG CUSTARD PIE	118
PEACH PIE FILLING	118
CHOCOLATE DELIGHT	118
APPLE BREAD	119
LELA'S TEACAKES	119
FRUITCAKE COOKIES	120
HAYSTACKS	120
POTATO CHIP COOKIES	121
CHOCOLATE COBBLER	121
PEACH COBBLER	122